Maya's Gold

Mary Vine

Windtree
Press

MAYA'S GOLD

Contact Information: info@windtreepress.com

Published by Windtree Press in cooperation with Melland Publishing, LLC.

Windtree Press

Corvallis, Oregon

http://windtreepress.com

Melland Publishing, LLC

Caldwell, ID

http://mellandpublishing.com

Published in the United States of America

Publishing History

1st Edition 2007, Black Lyon Publishing

2nd Edition 2023, Windtree Press

MAYA'S GOLD / Mary Vine – 2nd edition

Print ISBN 978-1-957638-61-4

Epub ISBN 978-1-957638-62-1

CHAPTER ONE

Stanton couldn't breathe and woke gasping for air. The room was dark and he didn't know where he was. He pushed the bedding away from his body and shot his arms out around him to get his bearings. After finding the bedside table, his hand grappled up the side of the lamp and switched it on.

"I'm okay. Focus, focus," he told himself, clutching a blanket with white knuckles.

His dream took him back six months to a hooded figure pulling a handgun from the front pocket of his sweatshirt. A bullet ripped through the shop window next to him, shattering glass fell everywhere and a store alarm sounded. The sounds echoed in his head repeatedly.

Stanton shook his head because he thought that living in the peaceful northeast Oregon town of Salisbury Junction would drive his panic attacks completely away.

He debated for the one-hundredth time whether he was wrong for not getting in touch with the police. There were no witnesses and he didn't get a good look at the man's face. Not much to go on. Not enough to draw attention to himself, a well-known writer, or to upset the quiet life he loved. No, he'd put it behind him and get on with his life.

The problem was he could not let it go. His personal sense of safety had been violated leaving him frozen in a strange suspended silence. It affected his writing. Editing took so much longer, afraid someone would take offense to something he'd written in a book and come after him.

Knowing sleep would not come easy, he rubbed his face with his hands and stepped out of bed. The moon shone through a break in the curtains. After deciding to take a walk in the moonlight, he dressed and put a small flashlight in his pocket.

MAYA STOPPED HER RESTLESS TOSSING AND TURNING AND STEPPED OUT of bed. The room was a virtual sauna and she could not tolerate it any longer. With little more than a shake, she slid her silk nightgown down the length of her body, then donned a short black terrycloth robe and sandals. After grabbing a flashlight, she headed down the hallway toward the backdoor.

"Come on, Wonder Dog. We're going for a little midnight swim."

The old Collie groaned, struggled to his feet and followed her outside.

The stars were brilliant, the moon huge and full. She smiled and took a deep breath of the heady night air. It smelled of summer—heat-parched ground and dry grass.

Only a slight breeze stirred and she wondered why the weather was already so warm here in early June. This was not what she remembered. No, it felt more like August and she hoped the last two days she had been here were not indicative of the usual northeast Oregon weather.

If she kept this place, she would get an air conditioner. *If.*

Marching through the pasture, trying to keep the hard dry grass from poking into her sandals, she followed the sounds of the rushing river with Wonder Dog panting behind her.

When she made it to the trees at the edge of the river she heard and saw what looked like a pickup driving by and turned off her flashlight. The moon was all she needed to swim by anyway. The current and depth of the river made swimming difficult, so getting wet and cooling off were her only priorities.

She hung her robe on a tree branch, and hopped into the cold water, letting out a yelp. Wonder Dog leaned down for a few licks of water, then went off into the bushes looking ready to recapture his interrupted night's sleep. She reminded herself to rouse him when she was done, otherwise he would probably be lying there until morning.

Crouching down, she let the cold river water run through her legs and up her arms. The exhilaration she felt made her chuckle, then sigh. She decided not to get her hair wet, as it would curl up and catch floating debris such as mud or twigs. She splashed her face and neck, and her body temperature cooled quickly.

The process took only a minute's time. At the precise moment she grabbed her robe, she heard something snap. Her heart picked up a beat and she fumbled, pulling the robe across her front. With straining eyes, she searched the bushes for signs of man or beast.

"What are you doing here?" She heard the firm male voice, then squinted from the shock of bright light in her eyes. Her heart sped up to a frantic drum roll, her only thought to finish putting on her robe. Knowing she would expose too much of herself, she clutched it tighter to her bosom.

Her attempts to dream up some sort of tale about a husband or father, or anyone likely to join her here soon, kept her from answering him immediately.

"I said what are you doing here? I saw a flash of light and wondered what you were doing on someone else's property."

She couldn't see him clearly in the shadow of the trees that lined the river.

"Are you the police?" Biting her lower lip, she took a few steps closer. Likewise, he did the same, but when he lowered the flashlight to guide his steps, she could see he was not in uniform.

"Stay back! Who are you?" she shrieked. She couldn't ever remember being so scared or feeling so vulnerable.

"The name's Black."

Maya stepped back. "I–I live here."

"You do, huh? I happen to know you don't. What's your name?"

Quickly she glanced around and realized she stood just off the property line and that could be the problem. "My name is Maya," she said, her teeth chattering.

He flashed the light down her figure.

"Obviously you can see I'm not out trying to cause trouble," she said. The light zoomed to her face making her blink and turn away.

"What? Are you bathing out here? Are you camping? Are you a mushroom hunter?"

Reality struck and with it the knowledge that if he knew anything about the area, he'd know that to find mushrooms you had to be in an area where the white firs grew, some miles from there.

The idea of his being a stranger to the area didn't comfort her any. She figured she'd use her tan skin to her advantage and admit to being a migrant worker, or mushroom hunter, or gypsy thief, or whatever she needed to be. She could just apologize and get the heck out of Dodge.

"Yes. I'll just go now." She quickly looked around and tried to figure out how to make a mad dash. He stepped closer. She backed up again, realizing he could be a rapist. If he was trying to get a better look, he obviously succeeded, since he took in an audible breath and sent another flash of light to her face.

"Don't be afraid," he said in a softer voice, then flashed the light across his own features.

He had dark hair and dark eyes. How she had a sagacious mind at this point, she didn't know. In other circumstances, she would have found him a very handsome man. Then, didn't serial killer Ted Bundy have good looks, too? This man had height, a good set of shoulders on him–and she wouldn't be much of a match in a struggle.

If she darted he might see her backside. What would happen if the sight of skin caused him to pursue her even more? If she could just get her robe on, she'd feel so much better.

She focused on making her voice come out even.

"Uh...Black. Mr. Black, please. I'll go now. Just turn your back and I'll put my robe on and be on my way."

When he didn't turn, she cried, "Please!"

He turned then and, in a flash, she was clothed and geared to sprint away when she remembered her dog. Now so old and hard of hearing, he was probably going to sleep right through her murder. "Wonder Dog!"

The man reeled and flashed his light into the bushes. She wished a fierce dog would come to her rescue, but knew better. She decided not to wait for Wonder. He could fend for himself. Seeing her chance, she tore through the trees and pasture as if the devil was in hot pursuit.

Thankfully, he was not.

STANTON BLACK WATCHED HER LONG LEGS FLEE ACROSS THE FIELD AND into the darkness and thought he must be dreaming. He shook his head and chuckled over the fact that he had a skinny-dipping beauty in his own backyard. The odds of this happening any place else he'd ever lived were nil. He suddenly grew serious, wondering if anyone knew he was in town yet. No, he decided, if it was a setup the girl wouldn't have left.

He rubbed his face and moaned. Tired, not only from lack of sleep, but also from the constant job of being on guard since becoming well known. He suddenly realized how paranoid he'd become.

After pointing his flashlight over an empty field, he decided to call it a night and headed for his newly rented house. Again he turned the flashlight where the little woodland nymph had gone. For a moment, he saw movement. After focusing his eyes, he realized it was just a dog, a Collie, in the field.

He shook his head as if to clear it. He had a job to do in Salisbury Junction and it didn't involve any young woman.

WHEN MAYA RETURNED TO THE HOUSE, SHE NOTICED THE LIGHT ON over the kitchen sink. She didn't remember turning it on. With a hand to her chest, she slowly stepped back to the open front door. Looking at the kitchen table, she spotted the bills she'd set out to pay in the morning. Hating clutter, she tended to stack mail and magazines in neat piles. The envelopes were fanned out on the table, like someone had picked them up and flipped through them before setting them down. Gooseflesh formed on her arms. Her heart started beating like it had at the river. With a hand to her ear, she listened for any movement.

"Oh!" she screamed. Wonder Dog had pushed against her legs trying to get through the door. "Oh," she said more quietly. Wonder sniffed the air then yawned and flopped down to rest.

She tried to convince herself that if there were anyone in the house he'd know it since dogs had senses far better than humans. Reluctantly, she closed the front door and patted her thigh to get Wonder to follow her through the house. He looked at her like he thought her crazy and rolled back onto his spine in his favorite sleeping position.

Several minutes had gone by and when no one jumped out to kill her, she decided to grab her book and head to bed. The book was closed, not open and face down like she'd left it on the coffee table. At least she thought so. She shook her head because she was being ridiculous. Surely, nothing was amiss; the man at the river simply scared her. He spooked her and she needed time to settle down.

Upon morning light, Maya literally shuddered at the thought that she might have been raped or even killed last night. She'd assumed she was safe out in this sparsely populated area.

She had no clue to the man's identity. After breakfast, she would ask her neighbor, Alice, if she knew him.

Alice was like a favorite great-aunt, a woman she looked forward to seeing every vacation her family had spent in Salisbury Junction. Alice might know what was going on in the neighborhood and who this stranger could be. If not, then they would look out for each other if he should return.

Yes, they would look out for each other, an additional reason for coming east this summer. Bereft of her parents, she desperately needed a sense of kin and Alice had always seemed a member of the family.

In anticipation of another hot day, she laid out a pair of Levi shorts and took a shower. Wonder Dog waited for her on the porch and strolled along with her when she left the house.

"Are you coming along to protect me again?" she asked him in jest. Even though he probably lingered to visit with the stranger last night, she still loved the old dog. Maya smiled when she thought of the irony of it all. This poor dog, which her mother made sure was a Collie identical to Lassie, received the glorified name of Wonder Dog. It was a wonder in itself that this ten-year-old dog made it to an upright position. She wondered why her father let her mother name anything. But, Wonder made a good companion and somehow she felt he understood her loss. He probably missed her parents, too. It was hard to believe that five years had gone by since her mother had died in a car crash.

She named her only daughter Maya and while not a bad name, saddled with the last name Valentine made for endless childhood teasing. Maya wondered if part of the reason her romantic mother married her father in the first place, was to get his last name. She sorely missed her mother now. Especially here at this house, a place she'd spent with her parents, many sweet summer days of her youth, before her happy family vanished like a puff of smoke.

IN A HOUSE NEARBY, ALICE ROBERTS SAT SHIVERING ON HER LIVING room couch. She shook so hard she wondered if she might die before she finished what she had been put on earth to do.

It wasn't fair. She had not asked for much in this world. Just to be able to pass on the history she loved so much in an extraordinary way. That was all.

Finally, she had gotten her chance. If only she could have had one more healthy day she would have succeeded, but now it was too late. She rolled up into the fetal position and coughed herself to sleep.

MAYA WALKED UP ALICE'S DRIVEWAY TO THE FAMILIAR GRAY TWO-STORY house and noticed flowerbeds filled with weeds. That wasn't like Alice, who took pride in her flowers and garden. Maya experienced a moment of dread when she knocked on the door.

No answer. She knocked harder, wondering if Alice had gone on vacation. As she turned to leave, she thought she heard someone call from inside.

Putting her ear to the door, she heard a frail, "Come in."

Alice's mortality had never crossed her mind. Now that it did, she didn't like the image it conjured up, not that the passing of a woman in her seventies would be a shock, but Alice continued to be a part of what she enjoyed about this country. She wanted her here always. It would be hard to lose another loved one. Not hard…devastating. She took a deep breath and opened the door.

Alice, with her small frame and white pixie hairdo, sat in her pink bathrobe on the flowered living room couch, a box of tissues at her side. Maya finally exhaled with the hope that Alice only had a cold.

"Maya," she said hoarsely. "I was hoping it would be you. I saw your car…" She gave a racking cough. "How long will you be staying? You'll be staying, won't you?"

"I'm on vacation. I drove in two days ago." She went over, leaned down and hugged her shoulder in greeting. Maya's eyes filled with tears due to a stirring in her chest she hadn't felt since the death of her father. She stood and turned away for a moment to gather herself. "I'll be staying for the summer."

Alice struggled to get up.

"Don't get up, I can see you're sick." Worried, Maya looked around the disheveled house. Alice was never one to leave her housework undone.

"Listen, I'm so sorry to hear about your father dying," Alice said. "He was a good man. I will miss seeing him here."

"Thank you. Yes, he was a good man." She took a deep breath to steady her emotions. "I miss seeing him, too."

"I thought it kind of odd that a doctor, a cardiologist would die from a heart attack at such a relatively young age," Alice said quietly, trying to keep from coughing.

Maya nodded, remembering the headlines: *Well-known cardiologist, Thomas Valentine, premature heart attack.* Maybe not so surprising. Some called him a type A personality, always busy, always working, always striving to prove something to someone or to himself. She'd learned from his mistakes. Special education was her major in college and she took a job with elementary students so she'd have her summers off. Time to live, breathe and enjoy life.

"But if I remember correctly," Alice said, "he was a driven man, perhaps because of his background, hmm?"

"Yes, as you know, the son of a gypsy woman." Maya put a hand to her face. "I know very little, only that he hated being put down because of his gypsy blood. People usually just think I have a great tan. I have his black eyes and black hair, but I'm two generations down the line and don't have such problems. He never talked about it. I wish now he had." Maya turned to look out the window.

Alice coughed until she turned red, yet still determined to get words out. "Hey, but on the brighter side it made him strive for wonderful things. Medical school and later considered one of the foremost leaders in his field. Tragic it really is, to have two parents gone and you so young."

To keep from crying, Maya mentally tried to squelch the sad thought. She was very good at it, having done it many times since her father's death.

She cleared her throat. "So, do you have a cold or something worse?"

"The doctor says I have pneumonia. I'm on my second round of antibiotics. It's just taking a while, I guess, with my age and all."

Maya could have stopped by the day before. She felt guilty now for not doing so and said as much.

"No. No, you didn't know."

"Well, let me at least help you tidy up." Maya turned into a white tornado, cleaning and picking up. She felt so sorry for Alice, almost to tears, with no relatives to tend to her. Alice, now a widow, didn't bear any children. Maya always thought that a shame since Alice had always been so good with her.

Maya remembered a time when she and her father vacationed here. It was just after her mother's death when Maya had taken ill and had a hard time recovering. Alice brought some chicken soup and sat with her so that her father could find temporary relief from his sorrow by riding his four-wheeler, fishing in the river and panning for gold. Maya needed a mother figure that summer and Alice filled it gladly. Now Maya was back, needing her again.

Maya did have her fiancé Jeff, but he'd left her for someone else when she couldn't get over her loss. The numbness that she'd harbored in her heart for some time came in handy when his engagement to be married was announced two weeks before she'd left for Salisbury Junction.

Alice slowly edged toward the bathroom. In passing, she stopped, smiled brightly and patted Maya's shoulder. Maya thought she saw a tear in her eye. She realized then that Alice needed her probably as much as she needed Alice.

When Alice enclosed herself in the bathroom, Maya stripped the sheets off her bed and put them in the washer. Low on detergent, she noted and decided it would be no big deal to make a shopping list for herself, plus one for Alice.

Alice smiled at the improvements but said, "This is no way for you to spend your vacation, dear."

"I have lots of time. I have all summer. It's a good thing since I can see you're going to need some help around here."

Alice grew misty-eyed again, but this time the tears fell. "I can't thank you enough."

"Your getting better will be thanks enough. Come sit at the table and I'll make you some oatmeal. Something nourishing to make you feel better." Sadly, oatmeal was one of the only things Alice had left in her cupboard.

"Oatmeal will be grand. All old people like oatmeal—you must have heard that," she said with a smile.

"I believe I heard that from you, that's why I thought I'd serve it," she answered with a wink.

Shortly, Maya placed the cooked oatmeal before Alice. "Listen, I happened to run into a stranger last night at the river, and it kind of gave me a start. Do we have any new neighbors around here?"

Alice thought for a moment. "No, same as it has been. Wait, Charles Johnson spends a lot of time in another state, now that he's retired and I happen to know he has a boarder."

"That's probably who I saw, since I was standing on Johnson's property when I, uh, saw the stranger."

Alice didn't say anything for a moment. She swallowed and started coughing again. After putting a napkin to her mouth, she said, "Black."

"Things are tough for you right now, but I wouldn't say things are black. Blue maybe," she said trying to perk the old woman up.

"No. Stanton Black, have you heard of him?"

Maya frowned and shook her head.

"You sure? He's a writer."

"Oh, yeah, the writer. Sure, who hasn't heard of him? What are you saying, Alice?"

Alice took a sip of water then continued, "Well, you know how I'm active with the Golden Years Historical Club. Stanton called when I was volunteering, saying he wanted to do some research in this area for his next book and wanted someone from the club to take him on a tour of some of the mining areas. He's from L.A. and needed a place to stay, so I told him about the Johnson place. Now he needs someone to give him a tour."

"I'm sure any one of the ladies would love to show him around. He'll be the talk of this town."

Alice nodded with a grimace and tried to finish the oatmeal. Maya left her alone while she tended to putting the sheets in the dryer, then spent some time in the bathroom cleaning, gathering towels and wash cloths to be washed. She felt very good that she made such a dent in the cleaning this morning and came back to the kitchen smiling.

Alice looked stricken, staring into her half empty bowl.

Maya's heart picked up a beat. "What's wrong, Alice?"

"Oh, don't be alarmed. I just should be well that's all."

"Give it some more time and rest. Now that I'm in town–"

"No, you don't understand, I'm supposed to give Mr. Black a tour of the area. Soon."

"But Alice, you can't. You're not well. Surely, someone else from the club can do this. How could they make–"

Alice held up a hand to stop her again and then started coughing once more. Maya refilled Alice's water glass and set it before her.

Alice took a few slow sips, looking up at her with sad eyes. "All my life I've wanted to do something special. Be someone special. What is better than to be part of a book, to help bring out this area's history?"

"Sure, I can understand that, but you can't help it if you're sick."

"That's where you come in."

"What did you say?"

Alice leaned toward her. "I've been praying for an answer and I think you're part of it."

Maya hated when people said that. How could she possibly say no if God said yes? Aside from that, she loved this woman.

"I'll help if I can. What is it you need, Alice?"

"You're right, Maya. Someone else in the club would be more than thrilled to take Mr. Black on a tour of the area. I want to be selfish just this once. I want to be the one to educate him on the area. I have so much to say. However, until I get well, I'm asking that you take him to a few places. When I get better, I can take over. I don't want one of those other old bats taking my last chance to contribute something special." Alice lost her voice. Maya needed to leave before the woman got so worn out she'd be in need of a hospital.

"If it means that much to you, of course. I'll get clean sheets on your bed, then I'll leave. I'll come back tomorrow and check on you and you can tell me more." Maya headed for the linen closet.

"You can't. He's coming today at two o'clock," Alice barely squeaked.

She must have heard her wrong–after all, her head was stuck in the linen closet and Alice could hardly speak. She righted herself and pushed her hair back behind her ear. "Say that again."

Clearing her voice Alice said, "He's coming today at two o'clock."

Maya sat down, sheets in hand. "But I don't really know a whole lot about the area. Only the few things Dad told me."

"You'll have to start with that." Alice stood up slowly and grabbed her head. "I also have some pamphlets for you to give him. That'll start you out."

She watched the sweet old woman search her desk and wanted to make this work. Somehow, she needed to persuade the man to wait around for Alice to recover. She would explain that nobody does it better than Alice when it comes to history. Good work demanded he wait for the best. If that didn't work, she'd think of something.

"I'll meet him here at two. You don't even stir. You need rest. I'll take care of everything. Don't worry."

CHAPTER TWO

*a*fter visiting with Alice, Maya searched through the pamphlets the older woman gave her. Looking at a map, she tried to remember all the things her father told her about the area. Stanton Black might be disappointed, yet only temporarily. Alice would be back on her feet soon to take over.

Carrying the pamphlets, Maya walked back to meet Stanton at two. She stopped and picked up what looked like a week's worth of mail out of Alice's mailbox, then continued up the incline.

When she reached Alice's home, she turned and looked back at what was now her property as stated in her father's will. The house wasn't much–a ranch style, two-bedroom home, gold in color with brown trim that needed repainting.

However, the house sat on the edge of a one-hundred-sixty-acre spread ten miles out of Salisbury Junction. The riverfront property included pasture, hills, pines and junipers, making it a beautiful piece and one that could add a lot of money to her purse. The money wasn't a consideration to her now. Even though what she made as a beginning teacher barely gave her enough to live on, her father had left her enough money to live a comfortable life if she invested well.

Though her house was not yet up for sale, a realtor told her about two prospective buyers. She needed to decide what to do about the place.

She sold her parents' home in Portland this past year and that wasn't too hard, but this place was going to be a different story. This was where her family came to relax, the only place her father *could* relax. He dreamed some day of retiring here to have time to find the gold that helped bring pioneers to this area over one hundred years ago. Not for monetary reasons, but for the recreation of it, poring over the earth with the search or panning for gold in the river. It was hard for her to think of selling his dream.

With a sigh, Maya laid her purse, the pamphlets and the mail on Alice's porch. She could focus on her own life once Alice got back on her feet and up to touring again.

Through the window, she spotted Alice napping on the couch and made a mental note to check in on her again after her expedition. Yes, expedition, in that much of the touring would be new to her as well as to the writer.

She hoped Black owned a four-wheel-drive, because the tour Alice had in mind called for it. She had left her front-wheel-drive car behind, not wanting to get it stuck out somewhere miles from a tow.

With ten minutes to spare, she stepped inside the flower garden encased in a seven-foot deer fence, and was bent over pulling weeds when he arrived. Problem number one taken care of–he drove a four-wheel-drive vehicle.

Standing up, she brushed her hands against her cutoffs. She watched him look from her to the house number, back to his paper work. When she approached his pickup, she saw recognition in his eyes. They narrowed for a moment before he opened the truck's door and stepped out.

This meeting was different from the last. She was fully clothed yet her heart picked up a beat. Not in a fearful way, at least not like last night, but she guessed the palpitating was due to his fame and attractiveness. The feeling reminded her of standing before an audience to make a speech. This surprised her since she was normally confident in herself and her capabilities, all but her tour guide abilities.

She couldn't ever remember staring at a man like she caught herself doing just then. Her gaze dropped to his muscular legs clad in shorts. When he cleared his throat, she looked up to see those same brown eyes she's seen last night, deep brown, nearly black. Her father's eyes were this color and that made her stare at them a moment longer.

"I thought you were a dream last night. Guess not," he said.

She let out a sigh. So much for her hope that he wouldn't recognize her. In response to her sigh, a momentary flash of amusement crossed his features, replaced just as quickly with a frown.

Standing straighter, she stuck out her hand. "My name is Maya Valentine."

"Stanton Black." He ignored her hand and his eyes narrowed. "What's this Valentine stuff?"

Most people responded, "Excuse me?" in response to her name, but not this man. This didn't earn him any points in her book. Her nervousness gone, replaced with the awareness that he was just a man and an impudent one at that. She hoped she could tolerate him for the time Alice needed.

She spoke, enunciating clearly and slowly, "My-uh, first name. Valentine, last name."

His eyebrows rose slowly, "Your parents would actually name you that?"

"Afraid so." She leaned up against his pickup. He looked at her lower torso so intensely that she immediately straightened, thinking he was worried she would scratch his vehicle. When he continued to look unabashedly, she changed her mind. He was giving her a male appraisal. Most men were polite enough to look when they weren't being caught at it, not so for him. She didn't like the size of his ego.

"Do you want me to turn around, so you can look at my backside?"

He lifted an eyebrow. "Sorry, I just thought a woman who skinny-dips probably wouldn't mind."

Shocked, she hesitated for a moment not knowing what to say.

He looked down at a piece of paper. "Where can I find Alice Roberts?"

"Inside, but–"

He turned from her abruptly, clearly dismissing her and headed for the door. She took a few quick steps and grabbed his steely arm before he could knock.

"What now?" he asked with a sigh.

She didn't like his tone and she wished Alice hadn't asked her to help. "Mr. Black, Alice is most likely sleeping and I don't want you to bother her."

"Listen, My Valentine, Alice and I are doing a little business. Go back to the river, or wherever you hail from and I'll just wake her. Rest assured she'll be glad I made my appointment."

This time she pulled his arm away from the door with a little more force. "Listen Black. I'm not your valentine and Alice happens to be sick. She can't help you now."

He stared at her. "Is she going to be okay?"

"Yes, but she needs rest."

He studied his paper again. "What was the name of that historical group?" he said to himself. He seemingly had dismissed her again.

Heaven knew she didn't want to say it, but she forced herself. "I'm your guide."

He looked from his paper to her face, shook his head and then looked at his paper again.

"Alice asked me to be your guide until she's back on her feet."

"Thanks, but I'll find out what the name of this group is and get someone else." He headed for his vehicle and she grabbed his arm once more.

Even though she'd like nothing more than to watch him drive away, she remembered how important this assignment was to Alice. Alice wanted the credit for this, not someone else in the group.

He got in the truck anyway and rolled down the window. Very businesslike he said, "What are your credentials? Why did she want you to guide me rather than someone else?"

Alice's reasons couldn't be made known. She bit her lip, unable to think of a reply.

"That's what I thought," he said, then started his truck.

She got in his face. "Do I look like a total idiot to you, or something? I happened to have gotten a 3.975 in college."

He turned off the motor. "Now we're getting somewhere. Your degree is in history."

She hoped she could get by without saying her degree *wasn't* in history. If he knew she was a special education teacher, he'd leave instantly. "I'm a teacher from Portland. I'm here for the summer. Alice asked me to help guide you until she's well. Who knows, maybe today will be our only day together."

STANTON HAD BEEN STUDYING HER FACE AND HER FULL LIPS AND HER long legs. Beautiful or not, he didn't trust her, no way. She had something up her sleeve. He figured anyone, not just a paranoid writer, could see she wanted something. Yet, he gave her points for determination.

Every instinct he had told him to drive away. It was just that he was already delayed nearly a day. He doubted he could get another appointment with what was left of daylight and he wanted to see what she was up to. He decided one day wouldn't kill him.

"Okay."

ALICE LOOKED OUT HER BEDROOM WINDOW AT STANTON AND MAYA. AT first she thought Stanton was going to leave without Maya and fear nearly paralyzed her. She grasped a rosary to her chest and prayed that this coupling would work. When Maya got in his truck, she coughed out a sigh of relief and thanked her Maker. Then she cried into the sleeve of her robe.

MAYA GRABBED HER PURSE AND THE PAMPHLETS. THEN RAN AROUND and jumped into the truck before he could change his mind.

"I'm driving?" he asked, eyebrows furrowed.

"Well, you see, I don't have a four-wheel-drive and we're going to need one. It's hard to say what kind of condition some of the back roads are in. Sometimes Old Man Winter can cause a little havoc."

"All right. Where to first?"

"How about a ghost town?"

He sighed and after a moment said, "Okay."

Maya looked through the pamphlets and found a good description and map to Greenhorn. "We'll go to Greenhorn."

At the end of the driveway he asked, "Which way, east or west?"

She flipped the pamphlet over and studied the map. "Uh...go left."

"You do know where you're going, don't you?"

"Sure, I just know left and right better than like, east and west." She winced and added, hopefully with a little more intelligence, "We'll need a full tank of gas and maybe a couple of sodas or bottled water, if you'd like. We'll come to a place about fifteen minutes down the road."

While Stanton used the restroom at the mini-mart, she tried to get information about Greenhorn out of the attendant. "Oh yes, Greenhorn. Can you wait a second for me to help this customer out in the back?"

"Certainly." Maya turned back to the counter and her eyes settled on a tabloid picture of Stanton Black with actress Michelle Karr hanging on his arm, looking at him like a woman longing for chocolate. His face held a serious expression, perhaps disappointed at their lack of privacy.

Maya picked up the magazine and brought it closer. Michelle Karr was a beautiful woman, she knew, as she'd seen her in more than a few movies. Just as light and blonde as Maya was dark and raven-haired.

"*A Summer Wedding?*" she read and then searched her mind trying to remember what she heard about them on *Entertainment Tonight*. She was familiar with him as an author, as she'd recently read one of his books. Now she was his tour guide. She turned to see the attendant approaching so she set the tabloid on the counter before her.

"So you want to know about Greenhorn, huh?" asked the attendant. "No life present, at least not year-round. Just a scattering of old buildings. However, it's worth seeing. What would you like to know about it?"

"Yes, what would you like to know?" Stanton asked from behind her. He set a bottle of water, some sunflower seeds and a cola, on the counter.

Maya closed her eyes and took a deep breath. "I was just wanting to know what someone living here all their lives had to say about Greenhorn, that's all."

"Oh, I've only lived here for three years, dear."

"Oh well, guess we'll go then," Maya returned with a smile.

Stanton picked up the tabloid and looked at Maya, "You want this? You actually read this stuff?" When he looked at his picture, he frowned even deeper.

"No thanks, but I'd like some water, too," Maya said. She went back, grabbed a bottle and returned to find the attendant flabbergasted that the author of the suspense stories she read came into her store. He waited a moment for the woman to return with her book so he could sign it.

While Maya watched his jaw clench, he caught her staring and said, "Are you sure you don't need to go to the restroom? Not too many more stops out in the wild. Then you probably know that, don't you?"

Somehow, she thought that a man sought after by a famous actress–and a successful writer to boot, might at least act happy. She couldn't blame him for his concern about her tour guiding skills. However, she was a human being and deserved a little respect. She lifted her chin and headed for the restroom. Maybe she'd find someone in there who knew something about Greenhorn. Alice owed her big time.

When she returned, Stanton was in the pickup, engine running.

The attendant looked up from the tabloid. "This article says a marriage might be in the offing for Mr. Black. Is this true?"

The woman was almost swooning because she'd gotten to meet Stanton Black. It irritated Maya to think others considered him perfect when he was not. "I'm just his mistress. He doesn't discuss his marriage plans with me," Maya answered and watched the woman's jaw drop nearly to the counter.

She chuckled to herself when she scooted up into the pickup.

"What's so funny?" he asked, a little testy.

Maya waited until Stanton backed the truck up, then made it back to the road. "Oh, I just told the woman inside that I was your mistress." She chuckled again.

He looked at her with wide eyes and a slack jaw. "Why the hell did you tell her that?"

"She asked if the tabloid was true. She wondered if you were getting married to the actress. I said you didn't discuss that part of your life with me, 'cause I was just your mistress."

"You have no idea what it's like to be in my spot," he said, gripping the steering wheel. "Believe me, a tabloid loves to gobble that kind of gossip right up."

She was about to say he didn't have a sense of humor, but then on second thought he could be right. She could have started something unpleasant. Truly, she was becoming nothing but trouble for him. *Let this day end soon and let Alice be on duty tomorrow.*

"Oh. Uh. Sorry. I didn't think that–"

His hands relaxed and he started to chuckle. Even though she felt a little guilty, she couldn't help but smile. For it was the first time she'd seen *him* smile. It lit up his face.

When he was quiet she said, "Well, are you getting married this summer?"

"Well, are you my mistress?"

He obviously didn't want to answer her question, but she wanted to know. Eyes squinting, trying to figure out how to play this game, she said, "Does one have anything to do with the other?"

"For most women, yes."

She didn't have the energy for the game. Besides, she was trying to figure out if they were traveling left or right, east or west. Yes, she decided, they were going the right way. He downed his cola, while she tried to get comfortable, folding her knees to her chin to stretch them.

"You have a beautiful skin tone."

She looked over at him, surprised. She'd assumed he preferred blondes, considering Michelle with her light skin and hair.

"Thanks, that's the gypsy in me."

"Really?"

She did her best verbal imitation of a gypsy fortuneteller and Stanton's face lit up again.

After a moment she said, "Why are you on this little tour?"

"A book."

"I know that, but you write thrillers, contemporary ones at that. So how does what you do fit in with the gold mining days?"

He seemed to be gathering his thoughts. She waited while they traveled deeper and deeper into nowhere.

STANTON WONDERED WHY SHE HADN'T APPROACHED HIM ABOUT MONEY yet. He thought that perhaps she was a budding young journalist out to get a top story. Yet, she didn't look like any serious reporter he'd ever seen. Reporters were always dressed for success. Perhaps that was part of her scam. Those shorts and legs could reel in any man.

He was not going to succumb so easily. He neither agreed, nor owed her a free story. "The murder takes place in the wilds of Oregon in a deserted ghost town. It was once a boomtown where you could just pick up gold along the creek beds. Now, where once laid gold, is the body of a beautiful young gypsy woman. Without any identification she lay beaten and raped and her throat was slit."

HE SOUNDED LIKE AN ACTOR AND WAS SO ENGROSSED IN WHAT HE WAS saying that it began to scare her. She didn't know this man from Adam. She once heard that some writers needed to live out a scene before they could pen it. They were so far away from civilization, it would take a while before anyone would find her. That is, if she could get away from him in one piece.

Her heart beat loudly when he pulled over and turned onto an old logging road. She sat up straight, put a hand on the dash and wondered if she should make a run for it.

"Relax, I just have to pee. I'll bet you thought I didn't have a sense of humor, huh?"

Well, she still didn't think he did. It wasn't funny and she told him so when he returned.

"Neither is reading that I'm engaged while I have a mistress."

She didn't comment, just looked out the window wondering if he, whom she thought of as a lunatic just a minute before, was engaged. She shook her head to clear it and then decided she was the one turning out to be a fruitcake. It didn't matter to her what he was as long as he fulfilled Alice's dream.

Her mind unwillingly went back to Stanton's engagement. How could Michelle Karr just send him off into the wild blue yonder without her? What if she knew he was miles from nowhere with a single female tour guide?

Jeff was engaged to her when he started seeing someone else. She shook her head. She detested that type of man.

Twisting the lid from her bottled water, she glanced over at Stanton again. He would be a temptation for nearly any woman, except herself. She now knew to be careful when it came to men. She even had a guideline that she followed. He wouldn't fit on her list. He was too handsome, too rich, too involved with a beautiful woman that most men drooled over. He was risky business for someone ordinary like herself.

"Why are you staring at me?" he asked. "It makes me uncomfortable."

Irritable was more like it, she thought. "You don't seem like a very happy man."

"Why should I be happy? I'm a long way from the comforts of my home in the wilds of Oregon, with a guide who apparently doesn't know a ghost town from a rat's behind."

Well, she couldn't argue with him about that. They'd been traveling for miles on a gravel road, but from the map on the back of the pamphlet she could tell they weren't lost and that the town should be somewhere up ahead.

"Don't worry. We're almost there." She tried to sound confident, then took another swig from the bottle of water.

"Hope so. I'm paying good money to see something."

Money? Alice didn't say anything about money. She couldn't help but wonder if perhaps Alice needed the money. Maybe it was part of the reason she wanted the job so badly.

"I'm not expecting any money," she said rather matter-of-factly.

"Then why are you here? Is it the interest in history?"

She felt like he was looking at her fearing she was some kind of groupie or obsessed fan or something. She certainly didn't want him thinking that. "I'll be honest. I'm doing this for Alice. Any and all payments shall be given to her."

"And you, being a teacher, can turn money down?"

"I have my own little stash of money. I teach because I love it."

"Of course. Where did you get your little stash of money?"

She looked at him and sighed. She really didn't want to share her life story with him. Why should she? She'd never see him again except on the back of one of his best-sellers. Luckily, she spotted Greenhorn. "Oh, look ahead! This is it."

She felt somewhat smug. Maybe being a tour guide was not so hard after all. The moment the truck stopped, she dashed out the door anxious to look around. In a moment, Stanton joined her.

"Look at this tree," she said, pointing to a tall, narrow tree with limbs going all the way down the trunk. "They are called white firs. Since you mentioned mushroom hunters last night, I'll tell you a little interesting bit I learned once. Edible mushrooms grow in areas where the white firs grow. You can gather them in season and sell them in Sumpter or Salisbury Junction."

"Is that where you get your money?"

She smiled. "No."

They walked to a large wooden sign that Maya read aloud. "Greenhorn City, established 1891 on Greenhorn Mountain. Two hotels, five saloons, three general stores, two livery stables, a meat market, city hall and jail, post office, an assay office, local newspaper, two blacksmith shops and a red-light district. Five hundred townspeople and over two thousand gold miners in the surrounding area. Greenhorn's 53.58 acres of private land at 6,500 feet elevation makes it the smallest and highest incorporated town in Oregon."

"I can read myself, you know," he said. "Ms. Guide, what does the sign mean by incorporated?"

She usually remembered what she read and she was never more thankful than now. "A patent was issued to the mayor making Greenhorn to create its own legal system. I believe it's the only document of its kind around."

Maya turned with a self-satisfied smile and followed Stanton's eyes to a large granite rock. "See the holes drilled in the top?" she said. "This is where the rock drilling contests were held."

She knew from the pamphlet this particular rock was on Main Street, which gave her an idea of where the town stood at one time. Of the few dilapidated buildings left, she wondered if one of them was the old Carpenter cabin that she'd read about. If so, it dated back to the early 1860s.

"How in the world did people ever even find this place?" Stanton asked while he took pictures. "It must have taken forever to get out here."

"My understanding is that they thought they could get rich quick whether by false advertising, 'cause newspapers used to lie about it, or with their own hopes. I guess that was enough to get them out here. Some people did strike it rich getting gold from the mines around here."

"Alice said the jail was moved to the Canyon City Museum," she added after a moment. "Uh–that's over by John Day."

Thanks to her collection of pamphlets, she told him some other facts and then left him to roam while she searched for a bush to squat behind.

On the way back, they stopped at Phillips Lake to stretch their legs. "Pretty isn't it? It's an award-winning reservoir. It's man-made, created by damming the Powder River in 1965," she said.

When Maya sat on a rock and looked out over the five-mile lake, her eyes grew misty. Many times she'd been here with her father. She missed him so much. She wished he were here with her now, gazing at the lake and telling her about the fish he'd pull out of it. A part of her was missing and at this moment it nearly took her breath away. Why did it have to happen? It was stupidly ironic that a cardiologist, outstanding in his field, should die from a heart attack. Why did he not recognize the signs and do something about it before it was too late?

"Are you okay?"

When she felt a hand on her shoulder, she rubbed her face and felt a little ashamed he caught her in such a state. "Uh–yeah. Principle fish are Rainbow Trout and Perch."

She now realized that seeing and hugging Alice earlier in the day had seemed to trigger the process of melting her numb heart. She sniffed again and when his eyebrows went up in question, she realized she couldn't tell him why she was upset without becoming completely undone. Instead she said, "Please tell me what you're going to be writing about. Why are you on this tour?"

STANTON HAD SEEN MANY FEMALE TEARS SINCE PUBERTY, BUT THESE tears were different somehow. He wanted to make them go away and punch out whoever caused them.

"I descend from a man who was a California miner and he came to this area in the early 1860's. Rivalry existed between the California and the Oregon miners. This relative was part of a group called the

Tarheads and the Oregonians were called Webfeet. Anyway, I've heard this stuff all my life and been fascinated with it. I understand California Gulch, where he mined, isn't far from the Johnson property I'm staying on."

"Sounds a little like fate to me."

"Yeah. I thought so, too," he said.

SHE GLANCED OVER AT HIM, CATCHING A HEART-STOPPING SMILE.

"I feel like I want to use my notoriety so that this era will not be forgotten," he added. "Take Greenhorn, for instance. What's going to happen to that place?"

She shrugged.

"It'll all be gone without even a marker, that's what. I just want to see it all first, then decide what I want to do."

"I see." Did she ever. He needed an experienced guide, a historian for that matter, especially for a work of nonfiction. Alice could help him, but Maya sure couldn't.

"Tomorrow I want to go to California Gulch and check it out." He looked at her, eyes challenging, as if he could read her thoughts.

She wondered if Alice would feel better tomorrow. Surely a little sightseeing wouldn't kill her.

He turned toward her and said, "When I originally talked to Alice on the phone, she told me that to get to California Gulch you would have to take some of it by foot. Some of the road is blocked off, so a little hike will be involved."

So much for a little sight-seeing. No way would Alice be ready for this. At least she remembered to pack her hiking boots.

CHAPTER THREE

*B*oomer limped around the edge of the Valentine property, twigs snapping beneath his feet and bushes brushing his thighs. His shoe caught on an exposed bit of tree root, sending him staggering forward before he regained his footing.

His curses rang through the woods. He cursed the United States government that had sent him to Vietnam where he'd lost half his left leg. What had he got for the years he spent fighting for his country? He'd wanted respect and recognition but instead he got ignored. They gave him a paltry pension that was barely enough to live on. The only attention he'd received was from the cops here in Oregon who busted him and the court that sent him for rehabilitation.

He spat on the ground. A whole damn year of his life spent in rehab before they figured they had straightened him out, and let him go. Well, he supposed that was all history and now he was about to capture the bluebird of happiness.

He was lucky-damn lucky to have met up with other dissatisfied vets. Lucky to have joined them in forming that survivalist group in Alaska where he learned the art of gold mining. Coming from a stint in Vietnam plus his adept blasting skills earned him the nickname Boomer.

Once Boomer returned to Oregon, he learned he especially wanted the respect of a good woman. Yet, he didn't have enough resources to impress the type of woman he wanted.

From other miners he learned of undiscovered gold in the eastern part of Oregon. Even though miners of long ago searched the area, gold still lay hidden. Precious metal that would earn him the honor not received, yet deserved from people around him.

He spent many hours searching maps and scouting out areas likely to contain traces of gold. At the age of sixty-five, he unearthed a streak of gold burrowed deep into the side of a hill. Nothing would stop him now, nothing or no one. He fought for his country and now he would fight for this gold. After all, he deserved respect, recognition and the woman of his dreams.

He limped forward, his gaze skimming the lush green fields surrounding the Valentine house and the blue-purple hills beyond. Soon, very soon, his ship would come in.

Boomer worked quite a while on the property he'd soon call his own. The adjoining house had been empty, leaving him free to do whatever he pleased.

Until Maya Valentine came back and that posed a few problems. None he took too seriously, for he believed she would be gone in no time.

She'd been over to visit her neighbor. He'd done a search on the neighboring properties and knew it belonged to an Alice Roberts. From what he'd witnessed, Ms. Roberts was alone and a bit of a hermit, since he hadn't caught her leaving the house. From this and after viewing the grounds around her house, he guessed she was elderly.

He'd heard the famous author Stanton Black was in town. Famous, he thought bitterly, when he'd done nothing to deserve it. Black hadn't done one blasted thing for his country. He deserved no respect.

One day he would have everything Stanton Black had, but the difference was he'd appreciate it.

As God was his witness, it was all working in his favor, since Black seemed to be spending time with Ms. Valentine. He believed with

Stanton's looks and notoriety, he would whisk her off in no time. In addition, she had a job in another city. The Valentine property would soon be rightfully his.

Boomer could almost feel the gold in his hands and he salivated at the thought.

He would call his realtor, that's what he'd do. He'd make an offer and she would accept. Everything fit together too well for her not to. He knew now more than ever before that it was fate that he should have this property, this gold, and the long-awaited respect. Then the last step in the plan, to have the woman he loved in his arms.

Now he would tend to business. He had digging to do and probably more blasting. *One step at a time*, he thought, *one step at a time.*

ONE DAY HAD PASSED SINCE MAYA'S TRIP TO GREENHORN. SHE STOOD, frustrated with arms crossed, over Alice sprawled out on her yellow rose printed couch.

"This is serious stuff, Alice. Stanton needs someone who knows this area and everything about it. I'm the last person on earth who should be going on a hike with him."

"Now I know what you're saying, Maya, but I'm feeling better. I'll soon be the tour guide."

"Yeah, but you're not well yet and he needs a professional now."

Alice leaned forward, putting her hands together in the lap of her pink terrycloth robe. Her face shone with the brightness of a woman enamored with a cause. "I don't want to lose this opportunity with Stanton Black. I know this area like the back of my hand and what more could I ever want than to help promote interest in the area I love so much?"

Maya sighed and rubbed her hand back and forth through her dark curls. How could she possibly deny this woman her dream? She scanned Alice's face, watched how she carried herself and couldn't deny that the woman was stronger today.

"What harm could there be in faking it a few more days?" Alice asked.

"A lot. The man's questioning my expertise. Besides that, he's so difficult."

Alice looked concerned. "What do you mean difficult? I found him to be nothing but professional in his dealings with me. He's not harassing you in some way is he?"

"No. Relax. He's not harassing me. He's just so arrogant. You know, stuck up. He doesn't care enough about me to harass me. He just wants a guide, a brilliant guide. So he has no use for me."

Alice attempted to clear her throat. "I don't understand why he wouldn't. You're so pretty that he'd have to notice you as a woman. You could give any woman a run for her money, if you weren't so choosy. And what a fine catch he would be."

Maya couldn't believe her ears. The woman was indeed desperate to think she'd have an affair with an engaged man. "You're not encouraging an affair, are you?"

"Only if your guide skills don't work. Oh, don't look so shocked, I'm only kidding. It wouldn't hurt to lead him on until I get my land legs again. I am better today. It's helped with you being back in the area. It's encouraged me. I'm so fond of you, you know, dear."

Maya smiled in response. While living in Portland, her best friend moved to North Carolina and until she established some new friendships, she felt the only other person she had in her life was Alice.

"Now you're just trying to butter me up, Alice, and it's working, too. I'll give it another day at least."

Alice clapped her hands to her mouth and coughed out a thank you.

Maya had spare time before Stanton arrived, so she walked back home to brush Wonder Dog and finish her book.

"My place," she said when they neared the house. It sounded so strange to her. This would always be her father's place and she wondered if she could actually sell it for that reason alone.

The house itself was not that spectacular. What was impressive was the Powder River that she could see from nearly every window.

Her father wanted to modernize and expand it with a great room and tall windows. However, that was her father's dream. She wondered when she would start dreaming again. She hoped soon as she hated this numbness she'd had within her chest.

But she was starting to feel again. All she could do was tell herself that by the end of the summer, just before school started again, she would have her answers, if not her dreams. Wonder Dog followed her in the door and headed for his water dish.

Maya pushed the message button on her answering machine. "This is Eve from A and H Realty. I have someone very interested in your property. Please call me at–"

Maya stopped the machine. This was not the first time Eve left a message. She'd told her that she needed more time. Her house was not even up for sale, for pity's sake. She wondered what kind of snake she was, to pester her like this.

In prepping for her hiking tour, Maya tried to decide whether she wanted to sweat to death in jeans, or whether she wanted to be cooler but scratch her legs on the bushes. She chose a long-sleeve shirt with a tank top underneath and then went with the cut offs, knowing she couldn't stand the heat. Then on second thought, she put a pair of jeans in her backpack.

She caught herself frowning at her reflection, deep in thought, while putting on her makeup. Even if Stanton fit every condition on her list for Mr. Right, she knew he wouldn't want a woman that turned out to be a counterfeit tour guide. He expected to be working with a historian, not a special education teacher. She felt quite guilty.

Her whole life she always tried to do the right thing. She saw why now. Life was far more comfortable that way.

"It's not like I'm robbing a bank or anything," she told Wonder Dog.

At least Alice didn't ask her to do that. Then she remembered she forgot to ask Alice about her money situation. Alice seemed to be doing this for reasons other than monetary, but she would ask her nonetheless. If Alice needed money, she could help her out. It would be money well spent. She'd have to remember to ask the next time she saw her.

Walking up Alice's driveway, she realized Stanton didn't even know where she lived. Probably a good thing. Then his lawyer couldn't find her.

"Besides, who would ever believe there was someone in the world named Maya Valentine, huh Wonder Dog?"

Wonder Dog danced in response then tried to catch up with Maya's pace. They both moved aside when Stanton drove up behind them. Maya walked around to the driver's side and smiled.

His hair looked like he'd put a hand through it and dark stubble began to form along his jaw line giving him a bad boy look that made her hormones do a little dance of appreciation.

She caught Stanton's eyes taking in her figure for a moment longer than appropriate, making her believe he found her attractive as well. He didn't return her smile but said coldly, "Is Ms. Roberts ready to escort me today?"

So much for Alice's idea of flirting. She tried to be patient with his rudeness. "Alice is better today," she said kindly, "but not good enough for a hike in the hills. She has given me a map and some instructions. I will be your escort today."

His eyes narrowed. "Is there really an Alice Roberts?"

"Certainly is. Tomorrow, she can guide you."

He frowned, but said nothing.

She crossed her arms and sighed. "Why don't you like me, Mr. Black?"

He sighed and reached for the door handle. "Get in." When she did, he added, "It's not that I don't like you, it's just that you don't ooze a love for this country."

"I guess I ooze quietly," she said and then looked out the window, lost in thought. He was right to want someone who oozed openly. Did she love this country? If not, did she ride on the coattail of her father's love? She hoped that by the end of the summer she would have answers to these questions.

The area was beautiful, yet different from the outskirts of Portland. There she would see the forests and much undergrowth. Here where they'd not get near the amount of rain, was less underbrush. Only at higher elevations did she see the firs. Mostly she observed pines and then dropping in elevation the juniper trees.

"Alice gave me this map."

Stanton took it from her, trying to read it and drive at the same time.

"Turn up here in a mile or so, at the Auburn Lane turn off. We'll be going by Auburn first."

He nodded and then laid the map down between them.

She said, "Did you know about a hundred years ago Auburn was the second largest city in Oregon, next to Oregon City?"

"Really?"

She was getting tired of the doubtful looks he cast her way. She lifted her chin. "Yes. A population of around six thousand people."

"Right now there are about two million people living in the Portland metro area, so that's hard to believe."

"I swear on a stack of Bibles," she continued with a hope that she would sound confident enough that she wouldn't have to swear to honesty each time she made a statement. "If you have doubts now, wait until we get to Auburn. There's hardly anything left."

He raised an eyebrow. "Then why are we going?"

That was a good question. "Because you need to see it for yourself." She was satisfied with her answer. He appeared to be, too.

"Tell me, I wondered all night what you could have been upset about at the lake."

This sudden imitation of caring surprised her since she didn't believe he could be so cold one moment and indulgent the next.

"My dog died," she lied.

"I saw your dog at Alice's–that is, if Alice really lives there."

"It's none of your business what upsets me," she said, voice rising. "I'm on the job when I'm with you and my personal business is my own."

"Not when you burst into tears on the job, my Valentine."

"Don't call me that."

He stopped the car near Auburn, or she assumed Auburn, expert tour guide that she was. Stanton turned off the engine. With his left arm draped over the steering wheel, he turned his body toward her. Obviously, they weren't going any further until she fessed up.

"My father died, all right?"

He sighed and then looked straight ahead. He shifted back into his seat uncomfortably and she derived much satisfaction from that. "Now aren't you glad you asked?"

"Sorry."

Once back on the road, she said, "Alice said we'll hit a patch of sagebrush just before going into the hills. When we get to the forest, we need take a right at a turnout. Looks like it's right up here. Yeah. See, there's the apple tree Alice mentioned. It was planted long ago." After a moment she added, "Did you think I was crying over some guy or something?"

"That was my first guess."

"Hardly. I haven't met the man who could make me care enough to blubber. On the job that is." She realized what she said was true, and for the first time admitted to herself that it was a good thing she didn't marry Jeff after all.

"Lucky girl then."

"Not so much lucky. I just recently decided not to let men consume my thoughts. I'm currently into meeting my goals, whether my education, or my job," she said simply, then looked over to see him staring at her.

"Oh, you're pretty young yet. Given time some dark, handsome guy will come into your life and you'll be swept off your feet."

Well, Jeff was blonde but he didn't need to know that. "Wait a minute. Dark and handsome, huh? I hope you're not referring to yourself," she said in jest.

"Or someone like me?"

"Ha!" she exploded. "Someone like you?" she said with a chuckle.

He did that thing with his jaw muscle, then pulled off the road into the turn out and flipped off the ignition. "What's that supposed to mean?"

Her laughter ceased when she realized she could be sounding rude. "I decided to go by a list of rules when it comes to men. That way I'm less likely to flub up."

"I don't believe it. I don't fit on this list?" he asked.

"Oh...no." She shook her head repeatedly.

"A list, huh? I've never heard of such a thing. What, pray tell, is on this list?"

This was a personal area to her, but then after today, she'd never see him again anyway. "Don't date men who live with their mother," she said with a smile.

"Good one. What else?"

"Don't date men who make less money than you do."

"Well that one shouldn't be hard since you're a teacher. But then your mushroom business is booming."

"Very funny." She laughed anyway, then added, "Don't date married men."

"Good one, too. Yet, I don't understand how I don't pass your little test. I can't believe you have a list, you know. A list sounds so dispassionate."

Shrugging her shoulders, she said, "Works for me."

"How don't I pass? I don't live with my mother. I make more money than a teacher and I'm not married."

"Oh my list contains more than three items. For you, Stanton Black, I'd have to say: Don't date anyone who's engaged."

"I'm *not* engaged." He pursed his lips in concentration. "Somehow, I have the feeling that there's something more."

"You're too handsome, too rich, too aloof." And she wondered if he was being completely truthful about Michelle as well.

"That's a crime? Puts me in a minority I guess."

"I'm being honest. If it weren't for this favor for Alice, I'd not give you the time of day." That wasn't hard for her to say, considering he'd not give her the time of day if it wasn't for Alice, too.

"Now look who's aloof." Then his eyebrows furrowed and he mumbled, "Favor for Alice?"

She decided she'd better not get into this Alice thing and quickly scanned the directions Alice gave them. "Start the truck again. Looks like we'll need to four-wheel it."

"What? We're not going to get out and walk?"

"Not yet."

"Okay, hold on."

They slowly followed the dirt road and found themselves on some of the worst roads she'd ever seen, damaged by weather and no upkeep. Maya gritted her teeth, held on to the door and kept looking at Stanton trying to gauge whether he thought the truck could make it or not. She hadn't a clue what he was thinking.

At this point she tried to figure out if she should tell him to stop, or continue along this treacherous path. They could get stuck in an area where cell phone service wasn't always accessible. She was holding her breath when Stanton stopped at a fork in the road.

"They've ruined this area," he said, and he was not talking about the roads. He looked out at the rows and rows of overturned rocks where miners searched through the ground to find gold.

He stepped out of the truck for a few moments and took pictures while she remained where she was to study the map.

"Left or right?"

The directions weren't clear at this point. She took a deep breath, chewed on her lower lip and then guessed, "Left."

"I hope you're right, Valentine."

It was hard to spot a graveyard with so many stumps and large rocks scattered through the area. She was about to confess her stupidity, with profound apologies for trying to be a tour guide in the first place, when Stanton spotted a wooden fence and the headstones beyond it.

She found an opening in the wooden fence that encompassed the front of the graveyard. When Stanton came around the back of the truck they stepped through.

She said, "This is what's left of Auburn, once the second largest town in Oregon. All the gold in these here hills could never have gotten me out here without a four-wheel-drive."

His eyes quickly scanned the area and settled back on her. "Yeah, but the people who came out here wanted to get rich quick. They didn't have your mushroom crop to fall back on."

"Or they weren't a famous author," she countered.

He turned then and frowned. "Speaking of which, how do I know you're not some groupie who's trying to get close to me by pretending to be a guide?"

"Ha!" She saw little flints of burning anger in those dark eyes, but she was much too bewildered by his remark to succumb to it. "Why in the world would you ever think that?"

"Skinny-dipping on my property for one."

Now she felt a little anger of her own. "It's not your property. It's Charles Johnson's."

He thumbed his chest. "I'm paying good money to rent that house this summer, so I'd say it's my property."

True enough, she thought. "Well, maybe I was looking for Johnson."

After turning his head from her, his head twisted back so far, she thought he'd be a good candidate for an actor in an Exorcist sequel. "You have a thing for Charles Johnson?"

"No." She wanted to add "stupid" but thought better of it. She took a deep breath to calm herself and then added, "I was extremely hot and so I went down to the river and found myself on Johnson's property."

After his eyebrows rose nearly to his hairline, she said, lacking patience, "Hot as in weather. It was a scorcher of a day and my house hadn't cooled down." It was best not to tell him she thought she was at the river on her own property. He didn't need to know where she lived.

"You know, I'd say a woman that lived by a set of rules would be totally boring, but skinny-dipping is not. I'm really intrigued at what all your list might include."

"It doesn't include skinny-dipping, because I'm getting air conditioning put in. How's that?"

"Boring."

"So be it. We're here to look this place over. Now let's focus."

"Not much to see," he said looking around.

"It is beautiful here though, absolutely beautiful."

They walked to the graves, abandoned to nature. "Alice says somewhere between twenty-five and one hundred graves are here."

"That doesn't sound very accurate. Quite a difference between twenty-five and one hundred."

She looked out across the area and scratched her head trying to remember what Alice said about the graveyard. "It's on half an acre and it was established in 1862." She thought that was the correct year. "I would assume records weren't computerized back then and wooden markers wouldn't have lasted."

That seemed to satisfy him. They came across a grave marked *H. H. Griffen*. She smiled because she'd done her homework on this man. "This is the grave of one of the first men who found gold in eastern Oregon. The story goes that he'd found it somewhere not far from here and they misspelled his name on the tombstone. His actual name is spelled, G-r-i-f-f-i-n."

"Fifty-nine years old. Sounds so young this day and age."

"It sure does." She thought about her father who was even younger than that.

Thankfully, Stanton seemed to understand her sadness and pulled her away from the grave. "Let's move on, think about other things."

They walked some more, and then she looked around for the hanging tree stump. The forest was full of stumps, so she scanned the area for the largest one she could find. She had no way of knowing if it was the actual hanging tree stump or not but pretended as if she knew when she told Stanton about it.

After clapping his hands, he sat down on the chosen stump. "If you believe that this is the same one, then I have this bridge I want to sell."

She ignored him. "Can you believe six thousand people lived here at one time?"

He glanced around. "Never could guess it."

"If you'd lived here, you'd probably have run the town newspaper," she said.

"Yeah, I'd probably have been too lazy to dig for gold. Too hard a job and life."

"And me. What would I have done?" she wondered aloud looking around again.

"The schoolmarm."

She shook her head. "Probably not with my gypsy background. The miners detested the Chinese, let alone a gypsy."

"Every town needs a gypsy fortune teller, doesn't it?"

"Oh, back then I would have probably been hung on this very stump for it."

"What's left then, besides being a hooker? You couldn't do that 'cause of your *list*."

She was sick and tired of his haughtiness and put her hands on her hips. "Explain yourself."

"No handsome, rich or aloof customers," he said counting off on his fingers. "Or married. Or engaged. You'd make very little money I'm afraid."

"Oh, I'm sure I could do well," she threw back smugly.

"Yeah, sure." He chuckled to himself.

She moved over to him, positioned herself over the trunk where he sat so that she stood straddled over him, making sure her bosom was nearly in his face. The move surprised him and he leaned back and studied her face.

"I could've gotten any man I wanted in this town, you egotistical son of a gun. And for my price. You know how I would've accomplished this?"

"You've got my attention," he returned, his eyes to her chest, and then followed her hand pushing the thick curls off her face.

She had blonde-haired Michelle in mind when she said quietly, "Because a man is a visual creature and I'm different. I'm dark and exotic and I have gypsy in my blood."

She seductively spoke some Bohemian words that told him he was a pig, and his heavy-lidded eyes locked with hers and held.

When she didn't move, he softly rubbed her legs and at that moment she was glad she wore shorts instead of her jeans. It had been a while since she'd seen desire in a man's eyes. She lingered longer than she should have.

A chipmunk scurried down a tree and ran across a path just a few feet from them. The spell was broken, at least for her. She stepped back, pivoted from him and absently ran a hand through her hair. She turned back to look at him and he smiled.

"All right, you win that one," he said, breathing loudly.

This was the first time she ever wondered if she should just chuck her list and jump into something foolish. She could turn around, go back to him and let happen what may. She was sure something would happen if she got in his face again. At this second, it almost didn't matter that she may not see him after tomorrow.

Sanity returned with each passing second. When she heard him clear his throat, she turned and put her hands on her cheeks, fingers splayed. "I'm sorry."

"Yeah, I had a feeling you would be. Let's get moving, Valentine."

She tried to explain when she followed him. "It's just that you get me going. You think you're so cool sometimes and it's hard for me to deal with."

"So getting me aroused was my fault, huh?"

She dodged broken limbs and rocks in her race to keep up with him. "No, I guess that doesn't really cut it. My actions are my own."

When he turned, she could see he was frustrated with her, like he'd like to leave her in the woods. Matter of fact, she could probably bet her new property he was thinking that. He turned and headed back toward the truck but stopped when she called his name.

"I usually have a reason for the way I think and what I say," he said.

"You've not treated me well. You–"

He directed an index finger at her. "I have kept you on haven't I? You're the one who has called me names. *Stuck up* and assorted synonyms."

"You've made fun of my name," she returned, hands on hips.

"*My Valentine,* is really bad, huh?" he said, his voice dripping sarcasm. "I do owe you an apology for that one."

Maya took a deep breath and tried to steady her rising temper. "All right, I admit that it's been hard for you not having Alice for a tour guide, but I'm doing the best I can. Please let's start over, okay? Let's just forget all this and start over."

"If I had a sense of humor I could do that, but then you don't think I have one, do you?"

"No." After a moment of silence, she spoke the same Bohemian words she had spoken before, only this time in a pleading tone.

Stanton obviously didn't know the language, for he grew solemn and shortened the distance between them. "Say that again," he said.

She put her whole soul into the words, as she believed he was a pig like the words professed.

Then he embraced her and for a moment she was frightened, until he gently took her lips in a kiss that deepened to awaken stirrings in the pit of her stomach. What a kiss. She couldn't ever remember seeing fireworks behind her eyelids like she did just then.

He stopped kissing her and pulled her even closer in a hug. His labored breathing sent her over the edge of sanity.

"What did you say to me? What was it you said?"

She absently said, "I called you a pig." Then she softly chuckled, while she searched for his lips again.

Stanton froze. She opened her eyes to a scowl. "You said I was a pig?"

"Well, you make me mad," she said, feeling justified, but a little barren when he stepped back from her.

"That's not fair."

She pushed her hair off her face. "What's not fair?"

"You were trying to seduce me with a few seductive words in a foreign language."

She crossed her arms and lifted her chin. "I called you a pig, ya pig. I was not trying to seduce you. Why would I want to seduce you? You're not on my list!"

Maya tried to stomp past him on the way back to the truck, but he grabbed her arm. "Because you're a gold-digger."

"I don't want your money. I have my own!" she screamed in anger with a little sexual frustration thrown in.

"Yes, your mushroom money. I don't believe it. I think you found out I was coming to town and you heard I needed a guide. For all I know Alice Roberts is tied to a chair somewhere."

"You writers have a lot of imagination, don't you?"

He sneered.

"I don't want you." She jerked her arm from his grasp and started toward the truck.

Now he dodged limbs and rocks to keep up with her. "A few moments ago you were nearly begging me to take you."

She didn't know how to answer that truth. Finally she said, "You just caught me at a weak moment, that's all."

His laughter echoed through the woods. She glanced back at him and thought it was too bad he looked so handsome when he was amused.

She shuffled her backpack from the seat of the pickup to the floor, to the seat, then back to the floor. "Take me home."

"I don't even know where you live. You could be from L.A., just following me around for all I know. Who are you really, My Valentine?"

She slammed the truck door, then paced back and forth in front of the hood, wringing her hands and wondering if she should spill her guts about Alice and possibly lose her friendship along with Alice's dreams.

Reopening the truck door, she reached then fumbled in her backpack until she grabbed her driver's license. She threw it at him.

He picked it up and read. "One hundred, twenty-five pounds."

"Very funny."

"All right. So there really is a Maya Valentine and you live in Portland. That much is true."

She nodded, smugly.

"It seems you live in an apartment, not a house. The mushrooms can't provide a house, hum?"

"I haven't decided on an area yet."

"I don't remember any teachers looking like you when I was in school."

"You don't believe I'm a teacher, either?"

"Tell me about the War of 1812."

He had her. History was not her strong point. She crossed her arms. "I wasn't born yet."

It didn't look like he was in the kind of hurry she was in to go home. He sat down on a different stump, quite possibly the real hanging stump, and waited for her to fess up.

"I graduated from the U of O three years ago. With honors. I'm sure that would be easy for you to find out."

He nodded but just stared at her, again waiting. She rubbed her thighs thinking maybe she could skirt the Alice issue if she brought up some other facts he'd wanted to know.

"My father was a distinguished doctor, a cardiologist. He worked very hard, so hard he put himself in an early grave. He left me with money, not the kind of money you have, but enough to make sure I have everything I need. He also left me with a house and a quarter of a section of land in this area. That is one-hundred-sixty acres. I can't believe I'm having to prove myself to you."

"Go on. What do you want with me? Besides sex," he added with a smirk.

Maya spit and then said "pig" again, this time in English. She was stunned for a moment when she realized in hindsight that her father had said his gypsy mother would spit when she was angry. There must be something to genetics after all. She didn't know where else it came from. "I would be totally happy to never see you again after this day. Your ego is so big it fills the forest. I told the truth when I said I was doing this for Alice. Alice is sick, but recovering, and she will be more than happy to take over where I left off."

"Do you mean with sex?"

Maya pointed a finger in his face. "For the record you don't have a sense of humor. You shouldn't be even thinking about sex. You have Michelle Karr to think of."

Finally, something she said made him mad. His face turned several shades of red. He stood up and put his backpack on. "I'm paying you to guide me, so guide me."

She felt better only because she finally burst through that shell of his and at least made him feel anger. She wanted the last word. "Okay, but I don't want your money."

CHAPTER FOUR

They drove down Old Auburn Lane, fruitlessly searching the map and the area outside their windows for signs of California Gulch.

"Should be some sort of marker put up," Stanton said. "This area is an important part of Oregon's history."

"I can't deny that. But the land you want to see is Forest Service land and beyond that, BLM land, so it's not like you need a marker to find a house." Maya knew as she'd made the proper telephone calls to be sure she wasn't going to be hiking around someone's property and get shot.

He frowned at her. "If you loved this area and history, you'd understand where I'm coming from."

For a moment, she braced herself and waited for him to tell her she wasn't a history teacher. When he didn't, she looked out the window and tried to see the area like Stanton saw it, or Alice, or her father for that matter. She did see the beauty, but she couldn't really attach any emotions to it just yet. Maybe this was how she'd determine if she should sell the property or not. Again, she told herself that by the end of the summer she'd know.

"A curve up ahead," she said, rechecking the map. "We're looking for road number three hundred."

"Yes!" Stanton displayed that gorgeous smile again. They traveled down Road 300 until they reached a roadblock. He parked and looked out over the area from the driver's seat. His smile faded when he looked at her. "You're not exactly dressed for traipsing around the forest."

"Excellent guide that I am, I'm prepared. See, jeans," she said, pulling pants out of her backpack. She unlaced and pulled off her hiking boots, in preparation for removing her shorts. When Stanton only sat, dumbly watching her, she cleared her throat.

"What? Oh, I've seen you naked before. Uh–at the river."

"Do you think so?" She didn't think he'd seen near the amount he wanted to, but she wasn't going to mention it. "Yeah, well this is daylight, so turn your head or get out or something. Peeping Tom's are not on my list, either."

"Boring," he said leaving the truck.

"Pig."

"I heard that," he said.

She grimaced, wiggled out of her shorts, pulled on her jeans and then left the truck.

They stood next to a creek in a narrow passageway between the two rocky slopes of California Gulch and Webfoot.

"It's got to be up this way," he said. "I want to climb up to the ridge and look over and down. It looks to me like this is the path we want to take. You lead the way, Valentine."

"Okay." Then she got a little nervous, thinking about the wildlife that could possibly live in this area. Big, dangerous wildlife like cougars and bears.

"What's the problem?" he asked.

"Oh, I was wondering if bears live around here," she said meekly.

"Probably the only thing that does. Don't worry, if we run into one, just fall down and get into the fetal position and put your hands behind your neck to protect it. Or if you'd prefer, you could call it a pig in a foreign language, then spit."

"Very funny," she replied, then marched off towards the ridge.

They were quiet for a long time, using all their concentration on taking cautious steps. After a strenuous walk, they stopped midway to share a bottle of water.

"I think I'll lead the way now," Stanton said.

"Why?"

"Because I'm getting tired of looking at your rear end."

She thought he was teasing, thinking he wanted her out of the way so he could move faster. She turned her behind toward him and looked down at it. "What, too big? Is it blocking your view?"

He looked away from her and said seriously, "No, they're nice hips. It's just not comfortable for me to be staring at them when I hike."

She smiled at that. The man admitted to a weakness. She couldn't believe it.

They started again, this time Stanton in front making it easier, since all she had to think about was stepping where he stepped. Except now she stared at his behind and it wasn't too comfortable for her either.

She never thought shortness of breath could be so sexy. Not her shortness of breath, but his when he turned to gaze down at where they'd been.

Again, she wondered about his relationship with Michelle Karr because lately she'd seen nearly as many pictures of Stanton and Michelle as she'd seen of Brad Pitt and his current flame. If they were indeed a couple, why wasn't she out here with him? She was evidently a trusting soul. Yet, Michelle was an attractive person and he left her alone in California. Maya knew she wouldn't like it if her fiancé was out in the middle of nowhere with another woman. Anyway, her special education students thought she was pretty.

At the top of the ridge they moved apart, each taking in the spectacular view of the rocky knolls, juniper and pine trees around them. Down below they could see tailing piles, stacks of rock the miners of times past searched through and cast aside. Trees sprouted from a top layer of soil covering many of the piles.

She turned and watched Stanton study the map then gaze out

across the land, determination evident in his features. She hoped, for Stanton's sake, they were on the right ridge.

Carefully she chose her words. "Yes, it's too bad the area's not marked any better. Anyway, you're seeing the same territory as your ancestor."

"Yeah." He must have liked the thought because he smiled. "It seems like it's taken me forever to get here."

He lay down on a grassy knoll, his backpack propping his head and shoulders up. Maya searched around and found a rock to sit on. Then she found herself watching his face, wondering what was going on in his head when he surveyed the area.

She gave him his space and then said, "Are you thinking about a book idea?"

"Sure, always." Then he added with a smile, "I'm thinking the murder of the gypsy woman should take place on this ridge. How about that?"

She smiled back. "Yeah, she said *pig* one too many times."

He squinted, "You almost called me a pig again, didn't you? I just barely caught your lips forming a P, didn't I?"

He was right, but she only smiled in answer.

"Come over here and call me a pig."

For a change, he was happy. Perhaps the adventure of being where he once only dreamed was intoxicating. It was contagious. After a moment, she placed herself in front of him, her heart picking up a beat in anticipation of fleeing after she insulted him.

"Pig!" she said with a giggle, but couldn't get away since Stanton reached out and grabbed her ankle. She lost her balance when he captured her arm. He pulled her down onto him, her back covered him and her hair was now in his face.

"I got you now," he said in her ear. "Now what do I do with you?"

She chuckled and said, "You wouldn't let anything happen to me, 'cause I'm your guide. Without me you'd never find your way out of here."

He laughed harder yet, allowing her to pull away but only slightly.

Then he pulled her up over his body and turned her over so that they were now face to face.

"You know you ought to smile more. It illuminates your face," she said.

His smile vanished, replaced by a thoughtful look. "In my whole life the only one who has said that to me is my mother. You must see me the same way she does."

She highly doubted that, but said instead, "Yes, and we both think you need a good whipping."

"Oh yeah, and just what do you think you can do to me?"

He loosened his hold and she pulled a leg over him. She straddled his abdomen, leaning over and pinning his arms over his head.

He chuckled. "What are you going to do, spit on me, Valentine?"

Now that she got the upper hand, she didn't know what to do and just stared down at him. She watched his eyes dilate and his smile vanish when he looked at her lips. Reaching out, she touched the base of his neck where his pulse quickened.

When his lips parted, her face flushed and she wasn't sure whether she was panting or trying to catch her breath. But she did recognize two things in equal measure, lust and fear, closely followed by the stark realization that she was smitten with him. It all added up to a futile infatuation.

"Well?"

"Well what?" she returned, still breathless.

"What are you going to do with me now that you've gotten me on my back? I could give you a few hints."

Albeit the lust was strong, but also the fear that he could hurt her. Even though this man could make her angry enough to spit, she knew she could care for him. So much so, that his vanishing after a one-night stand would be painful.

Maya wondered if this was what happened to Jeff, why he strayed, as the draw of a new romance could be intoxicating. She worked herself over to Stanton's side. "You've got to be the sexiest thing I've ever come across, but you can kind of scare me, too."

He pulled her to him as he had done earlier, her back to him with his face in her hair and gave her a strong hug. "Don't fear me," he said, and released her.

The hug was nice, but Maya wondered if she'd revealed too many risky thoughts. She stood. "Any gold to be found around here?" she asked, feeling self-conscious.

For a moment, he didn't answer, only looked up at her and sighed.

"Yes, you should know that being a guide." He stood and brushed off the seat of his pants.

"Well, sure I've heard that, but–"

"It's probably silly, but when I walk I find myself searching the rocks at my feet. I pick up the white rocks, the quartz, and look for streaks of gold in them."

She'd seen him do it. "My dad used to do that, too," she said, with a touch of melancholy.

After picking up a few more rocks and taking one long last look out at his surroundings, Stanton headed back down the ridge. She followed, mentally chastising herself for throwing herself at him the way she had. She'd have to say she was a little bit embarrassed. Now she knew the true meaning of the word tease, but she'd teased herself, too.

She was glad he was along, on the grounds that his guide would've had a little trouble finding the truck. She felt he probably knew that too, thus she spouted off a few more facts about the area that Alice had told her to cover her inadequacy.

Once in the truck, Stanton was quiet driving back, until he reached the farmland on Auburn Lane. "I'd like to buy some land in this area," he stated simply and then added, "I love this country. Thankfully, I'm a writer. I can live wherever I want."

Maya was envious of his knowing just what he wanted in life. She didn't know how to get there from here, so to speak. She knew she may have some land for sale soon, but since she was yet undecided, she saw no reason to tell him.

He looked at her as if waiting for a response. She said, "I know of a realtor. Her name is Eve. She works at A and H Realty. She's kind of pushy though."

"That's the best kind."

Once at Alice's, Maya decided she also needed to make a call to the pushy real estate agent. Looking out the truck's window, she could see a blue pickup truck parked in front of her place. A man walked in her front pasture, probably heading to the river to survey the property. Then Wonder Dog joined him with a wag of his tail. Since Wonder was not going to help her, she didn't know what else to do besides put up a no trespassing sign.

When Maya got out of the truck to say her last goodbye to Stanton, she saw Alice standing in the front entrance of her home. She waved them in and then stepped back when they entered. Alice wore a flowered shirt-dress and her short white hair looked like she had slicked it back with water and a comb.

"You must be feeling better, Alice. Uh–this is Stanton Black."

"At last we meet. I was beginning to fear there was no Alice Roberts," he said and shook her hand earnestly.

Maya rolled her eyes at him.

"Oh, of course there is," Alice said with a cough, then motioned them to sit down. "I've felt a little bit better today. I have some things I want to tell you."

Stanton sat down on the couch, but Maya decided to use her time wisely and straighten Alice's house. "Alice, I'll just start on these dishes. You two talk and I'll listen."

Alice seemed so eager to talk to Stanton about the history she loved that she hardly even noticed she was there. The lack of attention was fine with Maya, only glad that Alice was well enough to do this. Maybe now she could get on with her own life.

While filling the sink with soapy dishwater, she looked out the window and noted that the man was now getting into his truck and leaving her property. She didn't like this at all, someone traipsing around her residence without her permission. She couldn't wait to get home and call Eve to rectify the problem.

She heard Alice say she was sorry she didn't have anything to serve. "Do you want me to make some coffee?" Maya asked.

Stanton had been eyeing her carefully, then she saw that muscle flex in his jaw. She wondered what she was doing wrong now.

"None for me, dear. How about you, Mr. Black?" Alice asked, then covered her face with a tissue and coughed.

"No."

Maya took a clean glass from the cupboard and began filling it with water. "Then at least take this water, Alice."

"Thank you, Maya."

Maya stood by her until she quit coughing, then went back to finish the dishes. While Stanton listened to the tales of the California miners, she examined the contents of Alice's pantry and made a grocery list.

When Alice couldn't talk anymore for want of coughing, Stanton stood from the couch. "I must leave now. I'm very impressed with your knowledge of the area, Mrs. Roberts."

"Alice," she said with a cough.

"Okay, Alice," he said and smiled.

Maya was thankful Stanton prepared to leave, for Alice looked frail.

When Stanton left the house, Maya asked, "Do you want something to eat? Can I fix you something?"

"No, I had something before you arrived. I will just go to bed now. Thanks for helping with Mr. Black, Maya. For everything you do for me, period."

"No problem." Well, at least her comment was partly true. She didn't mind cleaning her house. "I'm going to the store in the morning. I've made a list for you, too."

"I hate to be such a bother. But, if you're sure it's not too much trouble."

"Not at all, Alice."

"Well then, can you pick up a prescription for me, too? It's my blood pressure medication."

"Absolutely." Maya helped Alice to bed and then wearily looked forward to going home and getting some rest.

When she stepped outside, she found that Stanton hadn't left after all. He leaned against the pickup, waiting for her.

"The way you were working I would assume you are Alice's housekeeper."

"You assume wrong. I'm only helping her out."

"You live in Portland much of the year, so how do you know this woman? How did you even know she needed help, if not providing a service?"

She couldn't believe how tired her legs were. They weren't accustomed to hiking, then coming back to clean a house. Now Stanton wanted to play a game of twenty questions. "You know, I'm pretty tired."

"I'm tired, too, Valentine, but I want some answers."

His stance caused her to believe she wasn't going anywhere until she told him what he wanted to hear. She sighed then said, "I'd do anything for Alice. She's been a summertime neighbor of mine for many years."

His eyebrows furrowed in question.

"I live over there," she said and pointed.

"Do you mean in the woods by the river?"

A little piqued, she stomped her foot. "No, there. That house."

His lips formed a circle, "Oh."

"Why is it you never give me the benefit of the doubt? Why don't you trust me?"

"Because you're a tour guide and you don't love history. Something else motivates you to do the things you do. I say that–since you don't appear to be a caring person judging by your treatment of me, someone you're working for, and yet you're trying to be Alice's savior."

That last remark stunned her into a moment of silence. He had only known her a few days. How could he make judgments about her? She deemed it impossible to truly know someone in such a short time. She thought about Alice and her eyes welled up with tears, but she fought them when her sadness turned to anger.

Through tight teeth she said, "My motivation is I want to help

Alice. My family is gone and I feel like she is the only one around who cares about me. Yes, unlike you, she cares about me. And I'm concerned that she looks like she's at Death's door half the time. And it's not peculiar to be a little reserved around some people."

His eyebrows were still furrowed, but he was apparently speechless as his jaw was open.

She couldn't resist saying, "No, I don't teach history. I teach special education." She started down the driveway, since this was her way of saying goodbye. She considered it better than a slap across the face.

Stanton came after her and turned her around. "Do you think teaching special education qualifies you to be my guide?"

The word "pompous" came to mind, but then she saw the humor in the situation and looked to the right, then to the left of him and tried to hold in her laughter. When she couldn't hold it in any longer, she laughed and said, "Yes."

He laughed, too. "Okay, you win that one, but I'm not through with you yet."

"What do you mean?" she asked slowly and cautiously.

"Alice's not completely on her feet. She said that I still may need your assistance."

"If I say no?"

He looked surprised. After a moment he said, "You won't let Alice down."

Before she could answer, he was in his truck and backed down the driveway. She wouldn't think about it now. She was too doggone tired.

CHAPTER FIVE

The sound of Wonder Dog trying to get into motion woke her. Maya lay at the edge of the bed, only inches away from Wonder's yawning mouth. She turned quickly. "Oh gee, Wonder Dog. All right. I'll get up and let you out."

Every muscle in her butt and legs screamed out when she walked to the door. She guessed she'd used muscles hiking that had been dormant all her life. When she opened the door, she heard a loud noise more resounding than a gunshot. She thought maybe it was thunder.

Wonder halted and then proceeded out the door when convinced nothing was on the other side. Maya looked up at the sky to find it clear and blue. The noise wasn't caused by thunder. She assumed it was the forest service, doing who knows what.

The first thing she did, after her coffee, was think about Stanton. He was wrong, she decided, saying she didn't care about people. After all, she did teach special education. He was only thinking of himself and the way she treated him. "Always thinking of himself, the egotistical pig," she told Wonder when he came back through the door.

He wagged his tail in agreement.

She shook her head and tried to focus on the day's proposed activities, which started with a call to Eve.

"A and H Realty. Eve Dole speaking."

"Yes. This is Maya Valentine."

"Oh, wonderful! I've wanted to talk to you. So you're back in town."

"Yes. I've been in town this week."

"Did you get my messages, then? I wasn't sure since you hadn't returned my calls. Lot of interest in your place."

"Ms. Dole, my house is not up for sale."

"Oh, yes, well, we can remedy that. If you could come down to my office–"

"No," Maya cut in.

"Excuse me?"

Maya rubbed her forehead and exhaled. "I haven't made a decision about selling my house, Ms. Dole."

"Oh, but you work in Portland, so I assumed–"

"No. Please, don't assume."

"I must tell you that three different parties have asked specifically for your place."

"Did you tell them the place was not for sale?"

"Well, no. I told them that the owner had died and he was the reason for having this house in the first place."

"*I* am the owner, Ms. Dole."

"Then last night that author, uh... What was his name?" Eve said as if Maya had not given any opposition.

"Stanton Black."

"Yes, thank you. He wanted your property, too."

"What do you mean he wanted my property?"

"Now he didn't say your property in particular. He just said that he wanted land in your area."

"That's why you're anxious to sell my property?"

"Well, yes, now you see why I'm excited about getting your property listed. Then again, you have the very type of property that could just sit for years and years because even though riverfront property is very desirable not everyone wants that many acres. What a stroke of luck this is to have buyers waiting in line. It's a rarity you must take advantage of."

Maya closed her eyes and shook her head. She should not have encouraged her with a comment. "I'm not listing it yet."

"Please, Ms. Valentine, let me tell you how much these parties will probably pay for your property."

"I'm not interested in the money." Well, Stanton wasn't convinced she wasn't interested in money and now neither was Eve. "Okay, Ms. Dole, here are the facts. My house is not for sale. Do not offer it to anyone even as a suggestion. I will be putting up a no trespassing sign and I will expect it to be honored."

"May I call from time to time to see if you've changed your mind?"

The woman just didn't get it. She knew now that even if she did decide to sell the property, she'd call someone else. "No. Don't call me. I'll call you," she said slowly. "Good day."

To take her mind off the conversation she'd just had, she grabbed the television remote and pressed the on button. A familiar face appeared on her favorite morning show. Maya leaned forward to catch the words Michelle Karr spoke to television newswoman, Victoria Ott.

"I'm very proud of this movie. I can't think of a better director than John Casey and the cast is talented and hard working as well," said Michelle to Victoria and pushed strands of platinum blonde hair up over her forehead.

Maya thought Michelle's facial features resembled model Christie Brinkley, with eyes that matched the color of a clear blue sky.

Victoria leaned forward and touched Michelle's hand. "I see a ring on your finger. I've also seen pictures of you with author Stanton Black. Have the two of you made any wedding plans?"

Michelle looked at her hand a moment, wiggled her fingers, and tugged at her earlobe for a second before smiling shyly. "Yes, I have been seeing Stanton, but he and I have agreed not to let the public in on our plans. When the time comes we don't want our wedding to be interrupted by photographers and newsmongers. I hope you understand."

"Of course. Will Stanton be with you at the awards ceremony next week?"

Michelle stuck out her perfectly formed lower lip. "Afraid not. He's working on a book project in Oregon and will be unable to attend."

Maya hadn't realized her heart was pounding until she'd turned off the television. When she considered Michelle's words a second time a feeling of downheartedness settled upon her. Somewhere deep inside she'd hoped Stanton was through with Michelle. After all, he said he wasn't engaged.

Standing, she set her mind to the busy day ahead. The disappointing, futile thoughts must be dismissed, especially since they would be like two ships passing in the night when Stanton realizes how worthless she'd be to a million-dollar book deal.

BOOMER ALSO WATCHED THE MORNING PROGRAM. HE LEANED FORWARD, smiled from ear to ear, and studied the beautiful face. He thought he was the luckiest man in the world to have Michelle Karr love him.

When Michelle flashed her ring and spoke of her relationship with Stanton Black, he went from light-headed happiness to shaking with anger that mimicked shuddering from the cold. Only when he saw her tug at her earlobe did he relax and realize that she'd made contact with him. He'd seen her do it before and it had become their special little way to communicate.

His mind flashed back to the first time he'd seen her over six months ago. It was the day he'd walked by a theater advertising a dollar movie night and decided to go in. Michelle's beautiful face filled the large screen and he let out a sigh that came from the depths of his being.

Everything about her enthralled him from the way she habitually pushed her hair back with her hand to every movement of her svelte body.

He wanted to know everything about her and visited the local library the following day. He read every magazine article he could get his hands on and felt such unusual passion for her that he came to believe that their souls must have known each other in another time.

His resources were limited, but he was determined to see her in person, to see if she felt the same connection. He drove to California the day of her latest movie premier and stood in the background that night. He stood for hours, waiting for a glimpse of her, but his wait was well worth it.

Her platinum hair curled around her face and neck in a 40s style, and her light green dress fanned out as it fell down around her ankles. Her beauty took the breath from his lungs. His breath returned, and frustration weighted his chest when he spotted Stanton Black getting out of a limousine to escort her.

Boomer shouldered his way through the crowd and stood so close to a cameraman that he could smell the man's aftershave. Michelle turned toward him and smiled. Boomer's heart pounded and then swelled when their eyes held. She winked and tugged at her ear the minute before Stanton pulled her away toward the entrance of the theatre.

The anger he felt at Stanton for breaking this connection their souls had made was humongous and he knew he had to get Michelle away from him. He'd make sure that Stanton wouldn't interfere with Michelle's destiny.

Stanton's publishing house told Boomer about a book signing he could attend. He took advantage of the crowded bookstore and stood unnoticed in the back, watching Stanton sign away a stack of books that towered beside him.

Towards the closing of the book signing, Boomer noticed Stanton eyeing the exits, and he studied his opponent like he'd studied the enemy in Vietnam.

Boomer left the store before the book signing was over and walked around to the back of the building, hid in the shadows and waited. When he heard the back door opening, he pulled the hood of his gray sweatshirt over his head and placed a hand around the gun in his pocket.

Boomer smirked. Stanton probably thought he was clever to outsmart the crowd in the bookstore. Little did the man realize, there was safety in numbers.

At first, Stanton didn't see him. But when he did, he picked up his step. Boomer had little time to take aim and cursed his artificial leg that made him limp and slow down. He took a shot and missed Stanton but hit a shop window.

Afraid someone had seen him, Boomer left town. He holed up north of L.A. in an old motel searching television channels for any news of an attack on the famed Stanton Black.

The only thing he learned was that Stanton and Michelle were Hollywood's hottest couple. The couple would be spending time apart. Michelle told the reporter she planned to be part of a film taking place in the Florida Keys, and Stanton's next project involved a trip to the historical gold mining areas of Oregon so he could research his next story.

Boomer stood, raised his hands to God in gratitude and laughed hysterically. The odds were great that Stanton would be in the very area that Boomer had decided to make his home. At one time northeast Oregon had some of the best hard rock mining in Oregon. This was no coincidence. Even a fool could see that God was going to give him another chance. God was going to deliver Stanton to his doorstep.

It was only a matter of time now before Stanton would be gone forever, and he and Michelle would be together as God ordained.

IN RUNNING HER MORNING'S ERRANDS, MAYA STOPPED AT THE pharmacy to pick up Alice's prescription. A blonde man with a beaming smile took her order. "Alice called to say you would be picking it up. Good thing she did, because I don't recognize you."

"Yeah, 'cause blood pressure meds really give people a good high," said Maya with a smile.

He wore a pin on his white jacket that identified himself as Chad. He looked up from his paperwork and smiled at her. "Yeah, can't be too careful, Ma'am."

When she received change back, Chad asked, "Are you a relative?"

"No. Friend."

"How is Alice? She's been sick such a long time," he said.

"She's not well yet. You'd think there would be some magic pill to help her." She bit on her lip becoming increasingly concerned about Alice's health.

Chad looked at the medicine bottle. "Dr. Rick Diethrick. Pretty good doctor."

On impulse she asked, "Where is his office?"

"Just around the block. That way," he pointed.

"Thanks, Chad."

She didn't think she would actually get to see Dr. Diethrick, but she thought maybe she could send the nurse back to ask him about Alice. She doubted any doctor would want to divulge personal information, but since she was here, she'd give it a try. If not, she would make an appointment for Alice and come in with her. Then she could ask all the questions she wanted. Perhaps Alice needed someone to ask for her, to be an advocate. Then again, could she afford to get any additional services? She was determined to find out. Just maybe, she thought, she could do something.

After only a moment of waiting, she was surprised to see the doctor come out and greet her. He nodded at her and said, "I'm Dr. Rick Diethrick. You're here about Alice Roberts." He was a man probably in his mid thirties with thinning brown hair and thick glasses.

"Yes, my name is Maya Valentine and I'm sorry to bother you. My father was a doctor, so I know how busy you are."

"Valentine? Dr. Valentine. Oh, the cardiologist who has a place around here?" he asked, seemingly impressed.

"Well yes, but he passed away this past year."

"Yes, I heard. I'm sorry. It's a great loss for the profession."

"Thank you. Anyway, Alice is my neighbor and I've been concerned about her health. I'm trying to care for her and want to know what else can be done."

"I must say I've been concerned she's had no relatives to care for her, so I'm happy to see someone's looking out for her now."

"I'm doing what I can. Yet she's still coughing and she's weak."

"She's a woman in her seventies, you know. Without the treatment she's getting, she could have died. Years ago that's how many elderly, and younger people for that matter, did die. From pneumonia."

She didn't want to ask, yet she had to know. "Do you think she could still die from this?"

"I don't know everything. She could die from complications from pneumonia, but I think if she rests and takes care of herself, she'll pull through. I'm very glad, like I said, that she has someone to help her out."

"If it was me and I had this illness, would that be your prescription for me, too? Or would I be having other tests done?"

"I understand what you are implying. If it was you, I would be concerned because you are much younger and if you weren't healing very fast, you see. Two different ball games here."

It made sense to her. She nodded.

"I've got to go now, but if you have some more concerns, bring her in."

"Thanks, Dr. Diethrick."

———

IT TOOK MAYA AWHILE, BUT SHE FINALLY FOUND A STORE THAT CARRIED no trespassing signs. When she finished grocery shopping, she drove to Alice's house and set her kitchen in order.

The older woman's financial status had been weighing heavily on Maya's mind. Especially after being at Dr. Diethrick's office, where she most likely accumulated some medical bills. Then Alice only wanted a meager supply of groceries from the store. After putting the groceries away, she set Alice's change on the table.

"Alice, how are you doing financially?"

"Oh...okay."

"Still, a little money from Stanton for your services wouldn't hurt, huh?"

"No, I thought you knew by now my interest in Stanton is not monetary," Alice said, sounding a little appalled.

"Work for pay is not a bad thing, Alice."

"That's right, but this is my donation to this county."

"Do you have medical insurance?"

"Yes, I have Medicare, plus a supplemental insurance. Don't worry about me, Maya. I'm fine."

Maya let out a breath, relieved to hear this. Now, how would she get Alice to rest enough to get well? She rubbed her forehead, then said, "I stopped by to see your doctor today."

Alice looked up from her rocking chair, still dressed in her night-clothes, with no more pep than when Maya put her to bed the night before. She looked worried.

"Oh." It was a word spoken with a measure of defeat added to it.

"He said you should make sure to rest and take care of yourself."

"I know."

"Don't you think it would be in your best interest then, to turn Stanton over to some other historian?"

Alice visually perked up. "What does that whippersnapper of a doctor know anyway? He's never been old. He knows nothing of what that entails."

"Okay, okay. Settle down." She didn't want Alice to get any sicker. Obviously, she wasn't thinking of giving Stanton up. Though Maya had planned to try and convince her to—ever since she met the good doctor. "Maybe if we just made a good sound plan then about what you can and can't do and kind of follow that. Hmm?"

"And I'm not a special education student, either."

"Okay," she said softly. "Okay, then what do you want me to do?"

Alice looked at the bags of groceries and then around the room. "I thank you for all you've done for me, but what I need most is your help with Stanton. Besides that, I don't care if the dishes pile up and the walls fall down around me."

Alice's eyes filled with tears. Maya's heart dropped and a lump formed in her throat as she watched the tears flow. If she didn't know it before, she knew now how sharing history with Stanton meant everything to her.

Maya's stomach clenched as she considered a new problem. If Stanton didn't come back, what would it do to Alice's health? She wondered how much Stanton would want to deal with Alice now that he'd been witness to her failing health. Maya knew she'd done what she could to help Alice, but it may not have been enough. Stanton was a businessman after all. He should, and could, afford the best possible guide. She knew his work was much too important to settle for less.

Maya sighed, feeling sorry for Alice just now. She wished she could wave a magic wand and make everything all right, but she couldn't. As it was, she did everything she knew how, except sleep with Stanton. Even if she had the morals of an alley cat, she doubted that would keep him around either.

"He seems interested in you, Maya," Alice said, as if she had heard her thoughts.

"No, he's interested in getting information for his new book."

"He stares at you. I've seen it with my own eyes."

Maya sighed in exasperation. "I'll not be a one-night stand, Alice."

"Don't take life so serious, dear. There's nothing wrong with a summer romance. You had them when you were a teenager, no harm in having one now."

"I've never been one to play the field, Alice. I need someone in my life who will love and commit to me. Not someone who's already seeing a beautiful actress."

"Yes, but finding someone is not going to happen if you pick and choose as carefully as you do. My goodness, I'd hate to see the man that would measure up to your yardstick. He'd be downright boring. Let me tell you right now, if you want a sensitive male forget it, 'cause if you find one, he's gay."

Maya chuckled at that. Alice smiled in return and then leaned her head back on the couch to rest. Maya knew she needed to scoot so she wouldn't wear Alice out.

"I'll continue to help but I won't compromise my principles," Maya said, opening the kitchen door to leave.

Alice closed her eyes. "I'm sure you won't dear."

WHEN MAYA CLOSED THE DOOR, ALICE HAD ANOTHER DREAM FORMING in her mind. Although she believed Stanton to be a good catch, Alice didn't think seriously about Maya and Stanton as a couple. Her main desire was that Maya could help Stanton stick around a little longer.

But now, the way Stanton's eyes settled on Maya made her know without a doubt that he didn't love someone else as Maya believed. If the man hadn't made comments during their conversation on the area's history, she'd have thought he wasn't listening at all.

Maya, who had lost so much, was only left with an old woman to love her. And all though she believed Maya to be the daughter of her heart, Maya was receiving far less than she gave. She was such a loving little gal, and she deserved to be loved by someone strong, smart and successful like Stanton.

Remembering Maya's words about her health made reality hit her full force in the gut. She'd spoken to her doctor and she wondered if Maya could have said something to Stanton about this. She shook her head to clear the negative thoughts, to hold to the belief that she could still be the one to spearhead Stanton's project.

Alice began to panic, finding it hard to catch her breath, afraid she met Stanton too soon. Now he knew how sick and old she was and useless to the project she so wanted to be a part of.

Alice went into the bathroom and coughed until she threw up. Then she made it to her bed where she lay wide-eyed with worry.

When Maya returned home, she had a bite to eat then grabbed a key hanging next to the back door and walked to the shed. She gritted her teeth while entering, thinking of all the spiders and mice that probably took up residence. Her mind flashed back to the many times her father warned her of the black widow spiders that were sometimes present in the area.

Maya found what she came for, the all-terrain vehicle, or four-wheeler, her father used to drive around the property. She intended to survey her land and perhaps gain some appreciation for it. Then she allowed herself room to reject the land also, wanting to just feel something and make a decision about it.

The navy blue ATV started and the gas gauge slowly went up. Her first effort was to get a feel for the machine. She lost Wonder Dog maneuvering across a small ravine. It took too much effort to go the distance, so he turned back panting toward the house.

Even a tour of the property proved painful, since her family had camped here many times over the years. She could almost hear the ghosts of their laughter in the noise of the ATV. She continued on to the corner marker her father had shown her so she'd not stray off the property. It took awhile but she found it on a steel fence post. She saw the lot numbers painted on each side of it.

Traveling west along the fence line, she spotted the remains of a campfire. She turned off the ATV and walked over to make a closer examination. Used recently, it still held the smoldering remains of a fire.

Maya clearly stood on her property, so another no trespassing sign was in order. She walked up a slight elevation and looked for further signs of intrusion. Nothing looked too out of place except a patch of dry grass, pushed down, perhaps by a tent. Then again, some deer could have used it for a bed.

Turning back, she spotted what looked like a small cave. She hesitated for a moment, wondering if it could be an animal's den, until she got closer. Then she saw the only way it could've been made by an animal was if he used a chisel, hammer, and explosives.

Just because the house remained empty most of the year didn't mean that someone could come and do what they wanted on her property. She hadn't a clue what to do about it. Maybe ask Alice what she'd do.

By the time she'd put up her one and only sign in the pasture by the river, she found it was nearly time for dinner. She made some burritos and then took them up the hill to Alice's place.

"Have you seen Stanton today?" Alice asked. She looked out the window while nervously twisting her handkerchief.

"No," Maya answered. She felt sorry for Alice but didn't know what else to do. She'd been wondering if her days with Stanton were over, and for good reason. Alice was sick and Maya was the tour guide from hell.

"Well, I guess I'm not surprised. I gave him plenty to read," Alice said and then sat down. The idea seemed to have settled her.

"Can I get you something else to go with your burrito?"

"How about half a glass of milk?" Alice said.

"Certainly." Maya stood up and walked to the refrigerator. "I took Dad's ATV, uh...my four-wheeler, out to look at the property. Someone has been camping out on the backside and they've blasted a hole into the side of a hill. It looks like a cave now."

"Oh, dear. I thought I heard some blasting this morning."

"Yeah, I heard it, too."

"Looks like someone's struck gold," said Alice.

"Gold?" Maya returned, dumbfounded.

"Well, what in the world did you think they were doing? This is gold country."

"I don't know. Some sort of vandalism, I guess. Somebody playing with explosives. I know it's gold country, but heaven knows I didn't think someone would be blowing up my property for it."

"What are you going to do about it, Maya?"

"I'm going to put up more no trespassing signs."

"Ha, that'll stop 'em," Alice said sarcastically. "You should report it to the police."

"Okay, I'll do that."

After Maya cleaned up the dinner dishes, Alice gave her some reading material. "Here are some things I think Stanton needs to do. Please look at these and be ready when Stanton comes back."

Maya took them. "Sure, Alice."

She couldn't tell Alice what she really thought. That Stanton wouldn't be back.

BOOMER DID NOT MISS THE ATV TRACKS. SOMEONE HAD BEEN investigating and he thought he knew who it was. If she wanted to get involved, then he would oblige. Besides, he'd been thinking that she was taking a little too long to go back home to Portland. He'd help her with that decision, too.

He followed her tracks to a point, and then walked quietly to her house. On closer examination, he saw that no one was home.

A woman was stupid to have a door like this, he thought with a chuckle. He broke a pane of glass in the door and turned the knob. He looked around himself and chuckled again. This was going to be fun. She'd be out of town in no time, then he could get all that he deserved. It would come none too soon.

WONDER DOG TRIED TO SNIFF MAYA'S FEET AS THEY WALKED DOWN THE hill toward home. She stopped to give him the opportunity, and then they were off again.

The heat was stifling, reminding her to make two calls tomorrow. Besides calling the police, she intended to call an air-conditioning company. Even if she decided to move, the air conditioning system wouldn't be a waste of money. It would only add to the value of her home.

She smiled when she thought of her last attempt at air condition-ing–skinny-dipping at the river and running into Stanton Black.

She stuck her key into the front door and nearly dropped the left-over burritos when she witnessed the devastation before her. Books were off the shelves, pictures tilted, couch cushions askew. In horror she stepped back, thinking someone might still be in the house. She plunked down her casserole dish and high-tailed it toward the road.

When she got to the end of her driveway, she spotted a pickup. It was Stanton and she frantically waved him over.

"Oh, Stanton! I don't know what to do!"

"Calm down. Calm down," he said, reaching out the truck window to grasp a hand. "Take a deep breath and tell me what's happened."

In the middle of a deep breath, she faltered, afraid now she'd hyperventilate. She pulled her hand away and splayed her fingers out on the sides of her jaw. "Someone has broken into my house. I guess I need to call the police. Yes, I need to call the police."

"Get in," he said. When she did, he looked in the direction of her house, took a deep breath of his own and said solemnly, "I'm going to the house and check it out."

"No. What if someone's still inside? And what if he has a gun?"

"Calm down. I doubt someone is robbing you for your mushroom money. Probably just some curious teenage boys broke in."

She thought he was only trying to make her feel better, but she still didn't think they should go back without the police. Yet, she'd guessed by now Stanton would do what he wanted to do.

He went in first and after a few minutes called her in. "Looks like someone broke a pane out of your back door then reached in and opened it." He turned to her, "I guess your dog didn't scare them off."

"No. He was with me. At Alice's." She couldn't believe what happened to her. She turned and surveyed the mess, dumped out drawers, things spread around. A lamp broken and a box of cereal had been strewn over the kitchen counter and onto the floor.

She wondered why out of all the people in the world this had to happen to her. With a grimacing frown and a hand to her chest, she became aware of being violated and sullied. Before she knew it, she was crying.

"Maya, try to calm down. Then I want you to look where you might have stored any valuables or money and see if anything's missing."

"Yes," she said with a sniff. "You're right. I didn't bring anything of much value with me. I brought a gold choker necklace and a few sets of earrings, but that's all. I usually write checks, or use cards for everything, so I don't ever have much cash around."

She headed to the bedroom where she found various pieces of undergarments spread across her bed. In panic, she ran into Stanton's arms and turned her face to his chest. When he said, "What in the–," she knew he spotted the underwear.

Taking a steadying breath, she turned from Stanton and looked into a small jewelry box.

"Any jewelry missing?" he asked, putting a hand on her shoulder.

"No."

"Do you have any important papers here that could be worth something to someone?" Stanton asked.

She tried to think for a moment. Stanton guided her out of the bedroom and into the kitchen where she grabbed a small box of papers and bills. "No. Anything of value is in Portland."

She walked into the living room and tried to straighten it up, but Stanton stopped her. "No, don't do anything yet. I'm calling the police."

"Thank you." She followed Stanton into the kitchen, afraid to be alone.

It took about ten minutes for the sheriff to arrive. A middle-aged man with short gray hair met her at the door. "Good evening. I'm Sam Crawford. Heard you had a disturbance out here."

She stuck out her hand. "Thank you for coming. My name's Maya."

"This is the Valentine residence then?"

"Yes."

"This is Mr. Valentine?"

"Heavens no," Maya said with a smile, but turned in time to see Stanton frown. "This is Stanton Black."

"Oh, you're that author, aren't you?"

Stanton nodded and shook Sam's hand.

"I heard you were in the area. Whoa, does look like you've had a problem here."

"Yes, someone broke in," Maya said.

"That does happen from time to time." He followed Maya to the back door. "Not the best kind of door to have, Ma'am. What's missing?"

"Nothing that I've been able to see."

"You might look in the bedroom, Mr. Crawford," Stanton said.

Maya stood in the living room, wringing her hands. When the two men came out, Sam sat across from her with a note pad and pencil. "Tell me about yourself, uh, Maya is it? Do you live here alone?"

"Yes, but not all year. I'm a teacher in Portland and I'm here for my summer vacation. I got here last week."

"Are you renting or do you own?"

"I own."

"Well, my first guess would be that someone was trying to check out an empty house. Thought that maybe you were still gone. Sometimes people rob these houses closed up for the year. One call I went on, someone cleaned a place clear out, toothbrush and comb included. Things like that do happen."

"Your second guess?" Stanton asked.

"After looking in your bedroom, I'd say some teenage boys were here on a lark. Unless you've got enemies, or something someone may want. Or a pervert is in the area," Sam added.

"Besides the pervert in the area–" She shuddered at that, then began again, "I noticed today when I went to the back of my property that someone's been camping on my land. Not far from this campsite someone has made a cave in the side of a hill. The area is clearly on my property. I was planning to call the sheriff about it in the morning."

Sam frowned. "Could be someone wants you to go back home and leave them to their newfound gold."

"This may not be connected, but I've gotten too many calls from a real estate lady who works at A and H Realty. She says she has parties interested in my property. The place isn't for sale and I told her that this morning."

"Could be related, but then maybe not. Could be the prospector's aren't rich enough to buy your property, just want the gold. Well, anyway, you've given me some food for thought. I'll check it out. For right now, nothing is missing, no one's hurt and I see only minor damage. You might try to find a way to lock up your place a little better, and let me know if something else comes up."

When Sam left, the first thing Maya did was grab the under things off her bed and put them in the washer.

Stanton watched her. "I'll help you straighten up then I want you to pack a bag. You'll stay tonight at my place."

Nothing she'd like better than to spend this night somewhere else. The cautious part of her wondered if it would be a mistake to go to Stanton's place and tried to consider her other options. She didn't want to spend this night alone yet she couldn't go to Alice's as she didn't want to upset her. She'd go with Stanton, at least tonight anyway. She believed she'd have a better perspective on this whole situation in the morning.

"Thanks, Stanton, I'll take you up on that."

"No problem. Just being neighborly. I'd do it for anybody."

With that comment, she knew he drew the line. She understood that, after all, he'd been dating a beautiful starlet. Someone as opposite to her in looks as darkness was to light.

CHAPTER SIX

"Focus, focus," Stanton told himself, as he did every other time he'd awoken disoriented. After touching the bedside table, his hand settled on a book he'd been reading and remembered where he was.

"I hate these," he said with a growl, then lay still waiting for his heartbeat to steady. Thankfully the panic attacks had come less often here in Salisbury Junction.

Knowing sleep would not come easy, he put his hands on his face and tried to focus on his work, on what he needed to do to get this current book done.

He remembered that earlier in the day he'd looked up the name of Alice Robert's historical group. He intended to call them in the morning. Although Alice was a sweet person with a lot of knowledge about the area's history, she was not healthy. No matter what her desire to help, he'd be putting her life in jeopardy by letting her work for him. He couldn't do that. Maya was not a professional tour guide, and until now he'd been meticulous at having every aspect of his career professional. However, that was before "My Valentine" stepped into his life.

Now, lying nearly naked one room from Maya, his thoughts were anything but professional. He remembered her silhouette by the river that first time they met and the way her backside moved up the hill during the hike.

He wanted to go to her, not even caring what the morrow may bring. She was the sexiest little thing he'd ever come across. In addition, he liked that spirit of hers when she was angry. He couldn't help but smile, visioning her spitting in anger.

He lifted his head, listening for any signs that would tell him she was still awake. If he could just go in and talk to her. But what would he say? That he wanted to sleep with her? He had too much pride for that. So, he'd go in and talk to her and get her to share. Women liked to have men listen to them. She would talk about the break-in and then she'd feel needy of him.

Lying back down, he sighed. Initially he'd asked her to spend the night in the spirit of the Good Samaritan. He couldn't be that shallow and heartless to take advantage of a woman in a tragic situation. No, sex with her was a crazy idea anyway. He would be gone soon and the spitting gypsy would only be a faint memory.

Still, while he lay awake for hours listening for movement, he realized she was not going to be an easy one to forget.

SEVEN HOURS OF TOSSING AND TURNING DIDN'T HELP MAYA COME UP with any clues as to who could possibly want to scare her off her property.

In the morning light, she stood looking around the living room at Charles Johnson's things–the furnishings, the knickknacks, and the pictures of his family. She'd never met the man, only heard his name mentioned over the years in reference to the neighbor next door. The décor was apparently Johnson's attempt at decorating his home with yard sale finds and matching pillows and paint colors, but he'd only partially finished. The antique wood pieces needed more sanding and varnish, but the timeworn green carpet was at least clean. This was obviously not Charles Johnson's main home.

Time was slipping away and Maya had plenty to do so she found it hard to wait for Stanton to rise. She stepped into Stanton's bedroom to say goodbye.

Asleep, Stanton lay haphazardly sprawled out across the bed, a bare chest exposed. Although a writer by profession, his chest was tan and his broad shoulders muscled. He had a smattering of hair across his chest that narrowed down to the sheet that lay just below his belly button. She dared not think about what lay beneath the sheet.

She gritted her teeth. What a beautiful sexy picture he made, she thought, and then decided to step out as quietly as she had come in. She needed to avoid putting herself in a situation she wouldn't want to leave.

"Valentine?" she heard.

"I'm leaving," she said in a whisper. "Go back to sleep."

He sat up.

She turned, hesitated for a moment and then headed for the door. "Thanks for everything."

"Just a minute. Are you sure you feel like going back? Do you want me to go with you?"

"I'm a big girl. I'll be fine."

"Wait. There's some places I want to see later. Could you be ready by, say eleven o'clock, to go?"

Apparently, he hadn't written her or Alice off and she knew Alice would be ecstatic. "Okay. Bye, then."

Eleven o'clock didn't give her much time, but at least she could make some headway into plans she'd made during the night.

The first thing she did was call to get a new door put in, one with no windows and better locks. She offered to pay the company more if they'd deliver that day, but she was out of luck. Tomorrow would be the soonest they could come out.

Until then, she didn't know if she could stay the night. A piece of cardboard and duct tape over the broken glass didn't make her feel very safe. She'd think about it later. Right now she straightened the house. It was as if someone had picked up the house, turned it over and shaken it. What she and Stanton had done last night hadn't put a dent in the work left to do.

She'd wished the officer had taken fingerprints or done something to make her feel like the case would be solved. On the other hand, in the scheme of things, massive damage wasn't done to man or property. She guessed she had nothing to worry about for now.

Nevertheless, she couldn't accept this. The whole situation with the underwear was just too creepy to let go. Maybe she was going to be the one to fix this problem and a few ideas formed in her mind. She'd start by leaving a message for Eve from A and H Realty.

Later, when Eve returned her call, Maya said, "Eve, glad you called back. I was thinking about our conversation yesterday and I believe I owe you an apology. You were just doing your job and I was a little short with you. I'm sorry."

"Oh, well, I guess I caught you at a bad time."

"Yeah," Maya said.

"Does that mean you're interested in selling your place?"

"I just think I need to know all the facts. You know, like how much money was offered, for one."

"Oh, sure. Let me get my file."

Maya sighed. Eve even had a file on the property she was not selling.

"Well, what do you want to know about?"

"Tell me everything," Maya said.

"Charles Johnson wants to buy your property."

She highly doubted Johnson would cause her any problems. He'd been a neighbor since her family bought the property. He'd only have to come to her and say if she decided to sell he'd be interested. That would be the neighborly way to go about it. She remembered Alice saying he lived most of the year in Arizona. He sounded harmless to her.

"Why'd he say he wanted my property?"

"Well, that's a funny question, Ms. Valentine. Real estate is a wonderful investment."

"Well, yes of course, but you mentioned other offers and I just wanted to be able to give the property to the best family, you know." She felt stupid after she made that comment.

"It's not like it's a child or even a dog, you know. It's only property."

"I know, sure, but I have some emotional involvement."

"Oh," Eve said, then was silent for a moment.

Maya tried again. "Any families with children?"

"Actually, no. Mr. Johnson doesn't have any children. But the other people-" Eve stopped, apparently looking over her file.

"Well, let me see. Of the four parties I know about... Stanton Black, you know the author, would probably get you the most money. I understand he's a rich man."

Maya thought about Stanton for a moment and then shook her head. She had no doubt if he wanted her property he'd just say so. He'd offer her a large amount to supplement her "mushroom money."

"He's single I might add," Eve said with a chuckle.

"I know, I've been spending some time with Stanton lately." Then mentally kicked herself for the comment.

Again, Eve was silent.

"Can you tell me about anyone else?"

Eve cleared her throat. "Why yes, a man from Northern California who would like to come to this area and open a mining store. He was up here looking this past week."

Maya wondered if the truck she'd seen from Alice's house belonged to him.

"The last one is a man from Salisbury Junction who came into an inheritance and he said he wanted to move out to the country. He was particularly interested in the river. He's single, but would like a family someday. That is, if you're concerned about children."

"Can I have the names, Eve, and where they live?"

Eve chuckled again, "I wouldn't be doing very good business if I gave the names to you without legally representing you, now would I? Then you could get all the money with no fee to a realtor. No, I wasn't born yesterday."

"Oh, I wouldn't dream of selling my home without a realtor." At least that was true.

"Well still, I don't think it would be to anyone else's advantage to give the names and addresses to you. Take Stanton Black for example, I doubt he'd want anyone to give out his personal information. I'd like to keep him for a client, you understand."

Now she wondered if Eve thought she only made this call to get information on Stanton. Probably especially since she stupidly mentioned she spent time with him. She didn't think she'd get any information now.

"I see," she said.

"Besides, you should be able to ask Stanton yourself."

"Yes, of course."

"I'm looking at my appointment calendar. When can we get together and put your house up for sale?"

"Not this week. I'm extremely busy this week." She didn't want all ties cut with Eve just yet. She still might think of a way to get the names out of her.

Eve sighed. "Then I'll talk to you next week. Good day, Ms. Valentine."

Maya looked at the clock. She was running out of time. She grabbed the information Alice had given her about the area and began reading. She groaned and wished she'd asked Stanton where they were going.

For that matter, she didn't know why Stanton just didn't go out scouting by himself. Her presence didn't add much and then with all the information Alice gave him to read, it was a mystery to her why he needed her.

"Alice sure is a high maintenance friend," she told Wonder Dog. He sighed appropriately.

When Stanton picked her up, he told her they were going to the library.

"What's so important at the library?" she asked, perplexed.

"Well, let me freshen your memory. As you know, being a guide and all, quite a bit of history is stored at the Salisbury Junction library, in addition of course, to the pictures. Some of the books Alice gave me to look at have pictures taken from the McCord collection at the library."

"Oh, yes," she said and rolled her eyes when he wasn't looking. "Of course. I thought you wanted to check how many of your books they keep on hand."

He frowned at her, but didn't say anything.

"I ordered a new door."

"Good idea." He rubbed his chin and then looked at her. "A and H Realty said you were asking about me."

She shook her head in disbelief. She honestly did not want anyone to know about the conversation she'd had with the real estate company, including Stanton. Her investigation was her own business. She rubbed her temples for she felt a headache coming on.

"You mean, Eve?"

"Yes. What do you think she could mean by that?"

"Why does everybody think I'm a stalker?"

"What?"

"Well, you thought I was a stalker," she said.

"I'm hardly everybody."

"See, you're not denying it." That irritated her. "For your information, if I wanted to know about you, I'd go down to the grocery store and buy some tabloids. Or read about you on the back cover of your books." She had actually meant to check the back of the novel she owned, but forgot.

"Very funny."

"I talked to Eve about selling my property today and your name came up, is all."

His eyebrows rose. "Eve told me about a possibility that you might sell. So you've decided to sell. You're not letting someone scare you off, are you?"

"I came here this summer to decide if I wanted to sell the property. I don't know what I want to do. I need some time to think. Nobody's scaring me off."

He chuckled.

"What's so funny?"

"Eve seems to think we're an item for some reason."

He stopped laughing abruptly when it took her a moment to answer.

"It's just that Eve lady, she makes me crazy," she said, her voice an octave higher. "She said that you were a single man, like I would care, you know. I just told her, in my own way, that I knew you."

He swerved to the side of the road and she grabbed the armrest. "In your own way? Why don't I just make an appointment for you with the *National Inquirer* if you are so set on destroying my life? Then why stop with just you? Eve could get a good fee for what she knows, too."

"All I said was that we were spending some time together. That's all!"

"That's all."

"That's all," she repeated.

She crossed her legs and moved them back and forth while she looked at him. She was ruining his life? She thought quite the opposite. If anything, this tour guide stuff was ruining hers.

"What is it about me that's dangerous to your reputation? Everything about me is average, except my little dab of gypsy blood. Is that it? Heaven forbid your friends and family should ever find out about me," she said, dripping sarcasm.

After a moment he sighed and said, "You're hardly average, Valentine. You just don't understand what it's like being in the limelight. I just want to keep my private life private."

She put her hand up. "All right." She could sympathize a little bit. She'd have to admit it would be tough to hear your beloved was off on a wild goose chase with a young female tour guide. "We've got to make some kind of truce here. We can just stick with telling people the facts. You're not romantically interested in me and I'm not romantically interested in you."

Now he held up a hand. "I didn't say I wasn't interested in you."

She still didn't think he had a sense of humor. "Well, you better not be when your heart belongs to another, mister."

"What are you talking about?"

"Never mind. Now, like I was saying, I can tell them I'm a teacher and I'm your tour guide."

"What do you think a good journalist would make of that?"

"It's the truth," she countered.

"The truth shall set you free, right? I can see we don't really understand each other, so let's just stick to business, alright? Let's focus on history, Valentine."

"Yes, the library," she said resignedly and rubbed her temples again. She wanted to ask him why he needed her at the library, but didn't.

The guide he needed was the librarian who pointed them in the direction of the Oregon Room where he found the McCord collection of photographs as well as other donated pictures. In addition, they found an old card catalog file detailing obituaries and other information, garnered over the years.

Stanton was like a boy in a candy shop, looking at the pictures and articles. She envied him for feeling strongly about something. It had been awhile since she had. Again, she wished all her sorrow would go away, so she could live life fully again.

"Maya, look!" He glanced around the library and lowered his voice. "Here is the same picture I saw when I was a boy. My relative, my distant cousin, see?" His happiness was contagious. Moreover, that smile.

"Oh, wonderful," she agreed and stepped closer to look at the picture. She focused in on the caption under it and then wondered if he'd shown this much excitement and pride when he first saw his own name and face in print. Stanton probably saw his name mentioned repeatedly in the press and became accustomed to it.

Yet, seeing this worn and torn picture of his relative thrilled him and for such a simple reason as being part of birthing a town.

"Why does this man fascinate you so much, Stanton?"

"I guess due to the type of man he was. Alice gave a description of the typical California miner. He was a pioneer and a man's man."

"You're a man's man. It seems it came out in your generation, too. I can imagine you going for whatever you want, Stanton."

He looked at her and smiled. "Thank you. But anyway, he stirs something inside me, you know, stirring enough passion to want to write a story."

While he elaborated on the thought, she realized she was one of the lucky few to get to hear the process of what it took to make this famous author create such phenomenal books. His sharing, along with his proximity to her, made her uneasy. Besides her attraction to him, her heart started softening toward him.

She closed her eyes and shook her head in defense. When she opened her eyes her gaze settled on his smile. His smile did funny things to her insides. She just wanted to lick his face or something. With an exhale she turned from him and grabbed another notebook full of pictures.

She came across a picture of five women taken in the late 1800s. The caption said they were dressed as gypsies, nothing more. Could it have been a play, she wondered, or Halloween get-together? Whatever they were doing it bothered her, not so much for herself as for her father.

The gypsy people who came before her actually did dress like that, lived like that and were made fun of like that. She had never thought of those things when she was a child, but now grown up, she did. She lost the opportunity to talk to her father about this picture and about his struggles to overcome any problems created by his heritage. She moaned and turned the page.

Stanton looked over at her then. "We probably should leave."

From the truck window, Maya watched the sun going down. The canopy of pinks, purples and oranges wouldn't last long. It would be dark soon. She found herself in the same predicament as the night before. She'd be going home to a dark house with a broken door and couldn't tell Alice about this, so she couldn't stay there. Stanton was the only other person around to whom she could turn to.

"Can I stay at your house one more night?" she asked, looking down at her lap.

While she watched his eyebrows go from his hairline to scrunching at the bridge of his nose, she decided that maybe a motel would be better. He could drop her off at her house and she could drive back into town. She didn't really like that her car wouldn't be parked at her home though, for its presence might prevent another intrusion. Then she remembered that hadn't stopped them the first time. Car or no, she would not sleep in that house tonight.

"I can understand your hesitation, Stanton. Maybe I should get a motel room."

"No, that will be okay. I understand. However I'm telling you right now that I'm in the mood to work tonight, so I won't be able to baby-sit you."

"Baby-sit me?" She was appalled.

He leaned back and apparently satisfied, smiled. "I bet you'd like to spit about right now."

She wouldn't give him the justification of knowing. "Don't be ridiculous."

He laughed aloud.

Talk about Jekyll and Hyde, she thought.

CHAPTER SEVEN

*M*aya packed an overnight bag. It only took a moment to grab it, and feed and water Wonder Dog.

She was relieved to see that nothing was disturbed. She wanted to think talking to Eve put an end to the break-ins. Perhaps now someone believed she would be moving and soon be gone. That might work for a while, she concluded, until that someone got tired of waiting for her to put up a for sale sign.

Maya chose to sleep on the couch as she had done the night before. She wore an oversized nightshirt that strayed from her shoulder from time to time, but otherwise modest. She took a lightweight quilt she'd gotten from Stanton and rolled up in it, then sighed, unwrapped and got up to see if anything on television could hold her interest.

After she found the remote control, she could only get three television stations that didn't come in very clearly. Obviously, Charles Johnson hadn't invested in a satellite dish, but then Alice said he wasn't here much of the year.

When she found nothing of interest, she turned off the television. In disgust, she flopped back on the couch. She should have brought a book to read, but she thought the Author of the Year would have something good to read lying around. Johnson only had decades old paperbacks lining his bookcase.

She listened for noises from Stanton. Occasionally, she heard him clear his throat or mumble. It seemed he was well into another best-seller.

Bored, she lifted an arm and started making animal shadows along the wall.

When the rotary telephone rang, she nearly jumped off the couch. She listened for Stanton, but obviously, he was not going to answer the landline. How could he just let it ring like that, without caller ID or anything? The curiosity would be too much for her. It was. She walked to the phone and answered it.

"Charles Johnson residence." Surely, she couldn't get into any trouble saying that. Stanton's bedroom door opened.

"Who is this?" the woman caller wanted to know.

"Who are you calling?" Maya replied.

"Stanton Black. Who is this?" she tried again.

Maya turned and handed the phone to Stanton. His jaw was flexing.

"Yes," she heard, then Stanton handed her the phone. "Magazine journalist. Do you have anything to say?"

She took the phone. "We are working on a book here. Stanton asks that all telephone calls go to his office. If you have this number, then certainly you have his office number. Good night."

Ignoring the frantic questioning, she hung up.

Stanton carefully took the wire out of the jack then turned to her, putting his hands on her shoulders. She could feel the warmth of his large hands through the thin nightshirt.

"All right, Maya, fess up."

"What?" she asked, then removed one of his hands to put her nightshirt back on her shoulder.

He backed her into the wall. "Did somebody hire you, or are you in this by yourself?" he asked, his voice rising.

She had no clue as to what he was saying. Her hand went to her chest. "I–I don't know what you mean."

"Perhaps you're a writer yourself, wanting to make the big story, *The two nights I spent with Stanton Black*. Or you wanted some real insight into Michelle Karr. Or maybe you're not working alone, but for someone else. Just how did that woman get my telephone number? Perhaps she wanted to make sure you really were here, huh?"

She dipped under his arm and out of his grip. "You're crazy, Stanton." She started to grab her bag, but Stanton pulled it out of her hand.

"Sure, no sex to write about but then, hey, you could be a married woman for all I know."

"That's ridiculous. Save your imagination for your books."

"Did you have someone mess up your house, so you could have an excuse to stay here, or did you do it yourself? Funny how nothing was actually taken."

The gall he had–to think that her nightmare was her own doing. She tried to step away from him, but he was too quick. He caught both of her arms and put them above her head and against the wall, then studied her face. In a moment, she would regain her momentum and pull away from him and go home. Right now she believed the lesser of the two evils was to go home and let someone break in and kill her.

"Just let me go," she said finally and twisted away from him. "I want to go home. You work the tour guide stuff out with Alice. I can't do this anymore. I have too many things to worry about as it is. I don't have it in me to worry about Alice and this, too."

"What?"

"You're too hard for me, Stanton. Your friendship is too much work."

"My friendship?"

"We just don't understand each other. We don't trust each other. If I were a guy, you'd have beat me up long ago."

He shook his head. "If you were a guy, you would have beaten me up."

She smiled at that. "I've told you all that I am. I am just a plain old special education teacher from Portland who lost her father and is trying to figure out what to do with the property he wanted her to have. Then I find Alice is sick and I want to help her get well. That's it. That's me. It's simple. I'm simple."

"You're far from simple, let me tell you," he said without a smile.

Maybe he knew all there was to know about her, but she knew nothing about him. He was extremely private and she couldn't help but feel he had something to hide. It was strange he never talked about Michelle Karr while she told the world all about the two of them on America's most watched morning news show.

Maya felt he was only interested in her because of her connection to Alice and because of her property, which he would probably like to buy. For all she knew he could be the one trying to scare her off. Yelling at her like a crazy man could do it.

Pointing to the door, she said, "I'm going home now."

He rubbed a hand through his hair. "No. Just stay."

"Do you believe me?"

"You can't go out now. Stay."

After they held eye contact for a few quiet moments, she wearily she sat down on the couch, looked at the quilt and sighed. She doubted she'd get any sleep now.

"Truce?" he asked. When she didn't answer right away he flexed his fingers repeatedly. "I think my hands are about done typing tonight. They're stiff."

"Rub the palms of your hands. That'll help."

He lifted an eyebrow. "How? Show me," he said and sat beside her.

"I learned this from our classroom's physical therapist. I have some students who need therapy on their hands." She took both of her hands and massaged his palm, making upward, circular strokes toward his fingers.

"Oh, yeah," he said with a moan, and closing his eyes he leaned back against the back of the couch. She gave both hands ample attention. When she stopped, he opened his eyes and observed her under heavy lids.

"I guess I owe you an apology."

"You guess?"

"I'm sorry. I just have the hardest time reading you."

"Likewise, I'm sure."

"Me?" His eyes widened.

"Yes, you. It's not what you say, it's what you don't say that holds the mystery."

He reached out to touch her face and she flinched away.

Finally, he said, "I want to go to Bourne tomorrow. Alice said I have to see the E and E Mine before the ruins are completely gone."

"Are you sure you want me to go?"

He nodded.

"I need to be around the house in the morning. After my door is delivered and put in, I can go."

"Good enough." He rubbed his hand through his hair. "Maya?"

"What?"

"Can we be friends?"

"I might be wrong, but I don't think so. Friends co-exist in peace. Why is it hard for us to get along?"

"I think I can probably show you, Valentine."

"What?"

He took her hand and put it on his shoulder. When she didn't pull it away, he moved in and kissed her lightly on the lips. It only made her want more. He pulled back and gave her that smile that caused lightness to her head and chest, and a smile that went clear to her ears.

"Just hold me," she said. She could deal with just that.

Stanton drew her head against his chest and then hugged her shoulders. She couldn't ever remember being hugged so thoroughly. Almost like he cared, really cared about her. She slowly rubbed his chest with the palm of her hand. Nobody hugged her these days. Even Alice was too weak to give her a good sound hug. It was nice. She'd have to remember to give hugs out freely to people who needed them and if that was the only benevolent thing she did in her lifetime, she knew at that moment it would be enough.

His heartbeat quickened and she looked up at him. "I can hear your heart beating."

"I don't have a heart," he said.

She chuckled. His heartbeat slowed and she reached up to touch his chin. She was sure it was many hours since he'd last shaved and it rasped like sandpaper. The stubble only added to his appeal, giving him an edge of danger. He also had the long, curling eyelashes that many women would kill for.

He put his hand in her hair and rubbed the back of her head. Now she knew why cats loved the gesture. She laid her head on his chest and her hand up under her chin. Her fingers splayed out and she could feel his washboard-like stomach, then pulled her fingers back in and listened to his breathing.

For some odd reason, she started thinking about her father and she started to cry. She tried hard to keep quiet, because it was embarrassing.

"Why are you crying?" he asked gently.

She waited for a moment to make sure her voice didn't break with emotion, but it didn't work. "I–I'm sorry. For some reason I was thinking about my dad."

He tightened his hold. "That's okay. I heard just today on the radio that it's called grieving. It has to come and it comes out of nowhere." He patted her back. "They said it means you're starting to heal."

The release made her feel better and she wiped at her eyes.

"Yeah, that's probably true." She hoped it was true. Sitting up, she tried to straighten the hem of her nightshirt, then pulled it down. Her efforts were fruitless, since it only displayed the full effect of her breasts. She noticed he didn't miss a thing.

"I suppose I'm keeping you from your sleep," she said.

"Yeah, like I want to sleep right now," he said with a chuckle, then rubbed the back of his neck and his gaze drifted to her legs.

Maya said, "You're wanting a physical relationship with me, aren't you?"

"I don't know that I want that, but I'm feeling it, yes."

"You know in the last twenty minutes, we've gone from accusing and yelling, hugging and crying, to wanting, uh–this. What a weird relationship."

"Sounds like a normal man-woman relationship to me," he returned and then laughed with her.

Maya could tell he waited for her to respond, to give him some kind of a signal to take this further. She looked away from him, vulnerable and wanting someone to care for her, needing the care even more than wanting sex. Looking at him now, that need was overpowering.

"You're still fearful of me," he said.

"Yes."

"I don't like that. I want you to be free-spirited with me. How can I make you not fear me?"

"I don't know. I'm willing to try," she said earnestly and leaned over and kissed him. The touch and feel of his lips was soft, yet pliable—not thin, hard and lacking. She'd give a lot to be able to kiss those lips every day for the rest of her life.

Perhaps therein lied her problem. Those lips were destined for Michelle Karr. Beautiful, talented, Michelle. Not descendant-of-the-gypsies, Maya.

If she had not lost her father recently, she wouldn't be so vulnerable and so susceptible to a hug. She wouldn't be in his arms right now. She would consider her list, shake her head and be on her way.

She pulled away from him suddenly.

"Don't tease me."

"You're right. I'm sorry," she said and stood up, her back facing him.

After a moment, he walked past her, shutting his bedroom door firmly.

Feeling very alone, she rolled up in the quilt and with a sigh, lay down on the couch. She told herself she would survive the loss of her loving parents and move on to a fulfilling life.

After these intense moments with Stanton, she tried to encourage herself by thinking of her special students and their all-encompassing love. Ms. Valentine was everything to them and she in turn showed them how to make their lives more successful. She didn't know how she would have gotten through the past months without them.

In her mind's eye she focused on their smiling faces until she drifted into fitful slumber.

STANTON LAY AWAKE, THINKING. HE REMEMBERED TAKING A BEAUTIFUL young woman out to lunch in Los Angeles. Besides liking the look of her, she was an intelligent woman, having just graduated from Harvard. He wanted to find out if she could possibly be someone he could be interested in having a relationship with.

The media found them before the entrée could be served and he didn't think he'd ever forget the stricken look on her face after she was asked some very personal questions. It didn't take her long to figure out she didn't want to be involved in something of this magnitude.

He couldn't blame her for wanting nothing to do with him from that point on, but it hurt him nonetheless. This led to the discovery that it was futile to even date someone at present and immersed himself in his work. That is, until he met Michelle.

"Maya, Maya, Maya," he said quietly, shaking his head.

Maya wanted to know about his relationship with Michelle just as much as he wanted to explain it to her. He wanted to tell Maya about everything in his life. What it was really like for him to be a famous author. The good and the bad, which included what happened to start his panic attacks.

Yes, Stanton wanted to trust Maya. He considered the ramifications of sharing his life with her, then sighed and rubbed his face with his hands.

But how could he dare tell anyone about that night? What if he told someone and it slipped out to the media? It would bring attention of magnificent proportions and he would be hard-pressed to forgive that person for letting it out.

He'd tried to school Maya on the subject of what to say to the public, but how could he trust someone who told too much to a mini-Mart attendant and a real estate agent? If she could easily talk about him to a stranger, then what would she say to an actual friend whom she needed to share her life with or who needed a favor? If Alice was any example of what she could do for a friend, then he could be in serious trouble.

His biggest problem concerning Maya was that she was unpredictable. She'd be easier to trust if she was predictable. Was she ever the same twice? No, not with him. She surprised him so much, he wondered why a fly didn't take up residence in his open-mouth astonishment.

He had to have someone he could count on. It was as simple as that. Otherwise, how could he get well? The million dollar question was: Could he have a healthy life with Maya, free from panic attacks while at the same time shadowed by the media?

CHAPTER EIGHT

$\mathcal{I}$n the early morning, Wonder Dog greeted her wholeheartedly, as if she had been gone for months. Feeling a little guilty for being gone so often, she handed him a pig's ear from a jar.

She smiled, thinking of her pig, Stanton. A pig, in that even though he was seeing Michelle he still wanted to be intimate with her.

"Men," she said to Wonder Dog. "You're a wonderful dog, because you always agree with me."

She checked her phone for messages.

"Ms. Valentine, this is Officer Sam Crawford. I was thinking about the sniper you've got on your property. That's what we call them–or claim jumpers. Anyway, it's best to introduce yourself to the intruder first. Then you'll have his name. Once you've talked to him and you're still sure you're in the right about the property line, then take it to court. I've heard of two deaths recently over claim jumping. Don't want to see anymore. You've got my number. Call me if you have questions."

She wondered what she was supposed to do besides go out and offer a plate of cookies. Sam was no help at all. Besides, she doubted that the sniper was any of her neighbors thinking they were on their own property.

She knew it wasn't Charles Johnson since he was in Arizona. On the other side of her was Alice. Just for her own knowledge, she would find out who owned the property behind her and call them.

Thankfully, the man arrived early to install her new door. In no time, the door was attached and ready to go, new keys included. She wasn't about to ever go through this break-in thing again—and that door would prevent another night spent with Stanton.

Maya ran her errands despite being tired from lack of sleep. She drove into town to get a cell phone, a pair of binoculars and a five-gallon gas container filled for her ATV.

When Maya stopped in to fill a prescription for Alice, she found Chad very talkative. He'd been easy to talk to and seeing many people each day, he was probably aware of any town gossip. She needed to find out who Eve was talking about when she said someone with an inheritance wanted to buy her property. She knew from experience that when someone got an inheritance people knew about it.

"Where's the local hangout?" Maya asked.

"That would be Princess Pat's. They've got good food, too."

"Well, I hardly know a soul and I think I might run over there some night and start to meet the people of this town."

Chad's smile reached his eyes. "My girlfriend, Mindy, and I could meet you over there anytime you'd like."

"That would be very nice. You know, someone told me about a miner who came into an inheritance. You see, I also came into an inheritance and think we'd have a lot in common. I've been given a house in the area. Since this is a small town, do you know who that might be?"

"Sure. That's Ryan. He's usually there on Friday nights." After a moment he added, "Special miner's night this Friday. Bet he'll be there. Hey, Mindy and I'll meet you there. We'll introduce you."

She just hated asking stupid questions. Never in her life had she acted man-crazy and she didn't want to start now. Yet, being a detective was turning out all right after all. If it would get trespassers off her property, then a little craziness was worth it.

Her last stop was to pick up some pita wraps and bottled water at the grocery store. A necessary stop since she doubted she'd find a hamburger stand in a ghost town.

She stopped at Alice's to get information about the ghost town of Bourne. With limited time, she did as much housekeeping as she could, then promised she'd stop by later to check on her.

Stanton arrived on time, grumpy as a bear. She could empathize. She hadn't gotten much sleep the last two nights, either. Today she remedied that problem, showing him the new door.

"Looks good," he said.

"I've also ordered some ornamental ironwork for the windows."

"Probably not a bad idea. That way you don't have to worry about the place whether you're here or in Portland." He turned from the door to look at her and rubbed his chin. "Tell me, were you satisfied with the sheriff's visit the other day?"

"Frankly, no. On television they always get the bad guys. But he did leave a message on the answering machine. I don't think he plans to do much of anything else."

"Well, I think he followed procedure. Just be sure that if you see something, you call him. Maybe if you hound him enough, he'll investigate a little further."

She turned, hiding her eyes from Stanton and said, "Sure." She'd already decided it was high time to handle things on her own. Become the liberated woman she believed she was. Anyway, she cooked up a plan far better than Sam's.

They headed west, or left as Maya would say, toward Bourne. Traveling on a gravel road, they noted the mileage marker since they were to drive out seven miles from the town of Sumpter.

She was thankful that moving deeper into the forest made for a cooler temperature.

"Stop," she said suddenly. "What's that?" She pointed to a cave in the side of the embankment.

"Well now you're the guide, Valentine."

She didn't reply, but got out of the truck and walked toward the cave, interested because it looked similar to the cave carved in the back of her property.

"You're not going in, I hope."

Stanton was right on her tail, probably ready to pull her back if need be.

"Of course not. I'm just curious," she said.

"Do I detect a love for the area?" He had apparently taken her personal interest as a historic one.

She looked back at him and thought she saw a flicker of hope in his eyes. She only smiled in return.

"You can't see very far inside," he said. "I don't see any recent tailings, or action here."

No, she didn't either, unlike the one she had at home. She looked back at Stanton.

He turned and gave the area around him a good perusal. "I guess gold is everywhere around here. I'd love to do a little digging and panning," he said, taking one last searching look at the entrance to the cave.

When they reached the town of Bourne, she put on her tour guide hat. "The main street here was the only through street because of the creek and canyon sides. Houses were built along the ledges. Let's see, the town was named after Jonathan Bourne, a U.S. Senator. A man like you who was once interested in eastern Oregon mines.

"I read one night the red light sector burned while the townspeople watched. The local pastor was the first man out of the burning building. He wasn't heard from again."

The smile he directed at her caused her to be thankful she did her homework.

"How'd I do?" she asked.

"Pretty good, Valentine."

Back in the truck, they turned a corner then got out and walked to the area Alice wanted them most to see. It was the old E and E mine. Alice had given her a photocopy of how the mine looked in 1900 and now they viewed the remains. It was an enormous structure, five levels of stone upon stone left exposed with the wooden exterior torn away. It was awesome to look at, as if it were the remains of a castle.

"Something's got to change. It's all vanishing," he said sadly. "Somebody's got to do something to preserve this."

They turned and walked back down the road, Stanton picking up rocks, searching for streaks of gold.

Some old buildings or homes were visible, a few barely standing, others in a heap. Amid them stood aged summer homes.

Back at the truck, she pulled the pita sandwiches out of her backpack.

Stanton's eyes widened with surprise. "You are certainly earning your money today, Maya." He pulled a couple of colas out of a small cooler. In a shaded area they found two rocks flat enough to sit on.

She tossed Stanton a couple of packaged condiments. "Remember, any money goes to Alice."

"Yeah, I keep forgetting about your mushroom money."

"I think Alice could use the money more than I could."

"You'd be happy just to live modestly, huh?" he asked.

"I suppose so. I'm not driven to riches. The process of having it all put my father in an early grave. I hope that I've learned from his mistakes. Some things are much more important than money."

"Then obviously nothing I could give you would make any difference."

"You can't buy friends, Stanton."

"I'd have to disagree with you on that one, Valentine."

"You can't buy me, Stanton."

Stanton swept his arm toward what was left of the town of Bourne. "What happened to your grandiose dreams of being a hooker in the good old days?"

She was indeed amused. "You mean gypsy fortune teller, don't you?" With a smile, she spoke the word *pig* in the language he seemed to appreciate.

He stopped chewing and looked at her void of a smile.

"Gosh, you're easy," she said and smiled again. "Wait till the tabloids get hold of the fact that a few words spoken in a foreign language turns your brain to mush."

He started chewing again. "If you were into getting rich they'd pay you a big salary for that information."

Toying with him she spoke the few other words she knew in other languages, mainly introductory words ending with taco, burrito and enchilada. He only smiled.

"Well, forget that theory. You're back to merely feeding your face."

"Never could read me, could you?"

Boy was he ever right. She took another bite of food.

"Fact is," he started and then swallowed. "Fact is it's you. You've got some magic about you that I'm sure goes back to your gypsy roots. That puts a spell on me."

"Yeah, right. Now why would I want to put a spell on you?"

"That's the hard part," he answered. "You enchant me but you don't let me near enough to do anything about it."

"That's not hard to figure out. Michelle Karr is the answer to that." Having suddenly lost her appetite, what was left of her sandwich tasted like cardboard. She stood up and moved to the edge of the canyon to end their conversation.

He was right behind her. "I think it's more than Michelle Karr. Something else holds you back. You've got to learn to trust me," he said in her ear. Behind her, he put his arms around her shoulders and looked down at the creek with her.

He tightened his hug and she closed her eyes, savoring it. His hugs were healing. She took a deep breath and enjoyed it. She didn't know when she'd get another from him, or from anybody.

He put his face in her hair and kissed her just above her ear. "You trust me up here, on this cliff, but that's as far as it goes."

She opened her eyes and looked down. She did trust him not to hurt her physically. Her feelings were what she couldn't risk. He could and probably would lambaste her emotionally.

"You don't share much about yourself. I have nothing to go on." She wanted to mention his relationship with Michelle, but couldn't muster the courage.

He tensed. "I want to be cared about for me, not for what I say or do."

"But, what someone says and does is certainly important."

The magic of the hug faded. She stepped away from him and the canyon and picked up her leftover sandwich. She downed the rest of her cola.

Stanton muttered something, glanced around the area and then picked up his garbage. "What are you doing tomorrow?"

Besides checking out the property, she planned to be helping Alice. "Why do you ask?"

"I just wanted to know if your tour guide service is booked up for tomorrow."

"I have nothing set in stone, except," she suddenly remembered, "I'm meeting friends for a drink tomorrow night."

"Friends? I wasn't aware you had friends over here. Girlfriends?" By the way he leaned forward and paused for her to answer, she'd swear he was waiting for her to utter the cure for cancer.

"Just a friend I've met recently."

His eyebrows furrowed and she wondered if he wanted her to be at his disposal until he was done in the area. She could understand that his work was of great consequence. He needed to know that she believed that, too.

"Stanton, I realize your work is important and I'll help you and Alice with this tour guide stuff. Be a gofer, or whatever. If you need time with me tomorrow, I'll make myself available. Just not tomorrow night, okay?"

Perhaps he didn't understand, since that telling muscle was moving in his jaw again. She thought she made herself clear, so she didn't know what his problem was.

He grunted and pointed to the truck. They were obviously going home. Fine with her since she didn't know what else to say about Bourne, besides making something up. She'd told herself long ago not to do that. Because, sure enough, she'd see her lie in print.

For miles he was silent. She closed her eyes and tried to rest. When he pulled up to her house, he told her he would not need her until Monday, since he had decided to go out of town for the weekend.

From the driveway, she watched him leave. She wondered if he was going to have a rendezvous with Michelle.

"It is none of my business," she told Wonder Dog and he wagged his tail in agreement.

CHAPTER NINE

The first thing in the morning, Maya rode the ATV out to the edge of her one-hundred-sixty acres to check for illegal gold prospecting.

As far as she could tell, no one had returned to the scene of the crime. The place was tidy, leaving no evidence or clues as to whom the perpetrator might be. She was hoping he'd left part of a package from explosives that would identify the name of the supplier. Not even a beer can left for fingerprints.

She knew nothing else to do, except find out who owned the property behind her. Yet, she highly doubted anyone would be stupid enough to think his or her property line didn't end at the fence. The fence was far from the site of the cave.

Her only real option was to meet Ryan Allan. She racked her brain for an opening topic of conversation. That would be the hard part, because she had to appear sane.

Maya decided not to act too eager for this introduction and arrive at Princess Pat's around eight o'clock. Which gave her plenty of time to doll herself up. She made sure her makeup was perfect and that her hair sprang out in just the right array of small ringlets, starting from the part on top of her head to down past her shoulders.

Over her underwear she donned an off-white sleeveless sheath dress that she thought displayed her gypsy tanned arms and legs nicely. She put a dab of perfume on all her pulse points. After she stepped into sandals, she smiled at her reflection in a full-length mirror. She figured if she wasn't pretty enough to gain Ryan's attention, then maybe she could offer to read his palm.

Maya felt nervous going into the bar unescorted. She'd never do that in Portland. However, she assured herself, this was a small town. Small towns were safer than larger ones.

The place rocked with country music. The crowd was an array of ages, probably from twenty-one to a few Alice's age. Many of the women wore jeans and sundresses, but a few were dressed up, so she didn't feel too out of place. It dawned on her, though, that she probably looked like a city slicker.

Some couples slow danced and even though she'd never danced with Stanton, she thought with a heavy heart how he'd held her. It was only yesterday that she'd seen him, but somehow knowing he was with Michelle made their parting seem distant.

She took a deep breath and looked about the room for Chad. He leaned against a log partition that separated the dining area from the dance floor, holding a beer and talking to a woman and two other men.

Not wanting to interrupt, she stood behind Chad waiting for an opportunity to present herself. His friend stopped talking in mid-sentence and his eyes widened when he saw her. Chad turned to see what he was looking at. Then did a double-take.

"I didn't mean to interrupt your conversation," Maya apologized.

"No, no. Hello, Maya. Maya, this is my girlfriend Mindy. And this is Johnny Olson and Ryan Allan."

"Hello," she said, and wiggled her fingers at Mindy, a petite young woman with straight auburn hair that reached to her waist. Maya smiled at Johnny, an older gentleman, and then looked over to Ryan. He had tawny hair, which curled up at the collar of his light blue Levi shirt. She guessed his age to be around thirty, but the lines on his face told of a hard life. It gave him an appealing, bad boy look.

She held fast to Chad's side, while deciding what to say to Ryan. What she'd practiced didn't seem to fit the moment.

Mindy stepped closer. "Why aren't you all dancing? I'm taking Chad. Ryan, why don't you take my new friend, Maya?"

Maya was relieved that Mindy suggested she dance with Ryan. She owed her one for this.

"That all right with you?" Ryan asked Maya.

She nodded and then looked at the others on the dance floor. Luckily, it was a slow dance. She did not know how to do country western dancing.

She appreciated that Ryan was proper and didn't hold her too close and she tried to keep eye contact when they talked. Some other place, some other time, she may have been interested in getting to know him better. Somehow, what little she knew made her extremely leery, not to mention he looked like one tough cookie.

"I haven't seen you around town. Are you visiting?" Ryan asked.

"Actually, I live in Portland. I have a house here, too. I'm a teacher so I have my summers off. What about you? Have you lived here long?"

"No, less than a year."

That surprised her. "Oh?"

"I'm from northern California."

"What brought you here?"

His blue eyes twinkled when he smiled. "Gold country. I might ask you the same thing."

"Gold country," she returned with a smile and then chuckled.

The music ended and he asked if she'd like to sit down. Again, she nodded. He guided her to two empty bar stools. She took the end seat.

"Really," she said. "My father bought a place here for that reason. He recently passed away so I've inherited it and now I'm trying to decide what I want to do with it."

Since Maya believed Ryan was the prospective A and H Realty client who had come into an inheritance, she waited for him to say that he lost someone, too. He didn't. He just looked around the room and then ended his glance with a smile at her.

She said, "It's been hard losing someone so close."

"I'm sorry about your loss," he said.

Again, he didn't take the bait. She nervously swerved the bar seat to the music.

"So are you getting any?" she asked.

"I beg your pardon?" he asked, eyes widening.

"Gold." She put her hand on her chest and chuckled. "Are you getting any gold?"

Amused he shook his head. "I've done a little searching in the Forest Service's designated areas. Got some clinkers."

She raised an eyebrow in question.

"A very small piece of gold," he explained. "But large enough to make a clinking sound when it hits the bottom of a gold pan."

"Oh." The music picked up and patrons line danced. She leaned closer to Ryan to make conversation easier over the loud music. He didn't move. He let her get close. His grin made her think he was happy with the situation.

"Well, anyway, I'm a special education teacher. Primary classroom." She crossed her legs and his gaze settled on them for a moment.

"Sounds like a tough job."

"Oh, I like it. There's a job for every kind of personality and it fits mine. What do you do, Ryan?"

"Do you want a drink?" he asked when the bartender stood in front of them.

"Oh, a Cola for me, please."

"Give me a shot of tequila with salt and lemon."

A red flag went up for Maya because she always thought an order of Tequila meant a preparation for a good time. She would have to be extremely careful not to let him think she was going to be his evening's amusement. She bit her lip, then turned and watched the dancers. They waited only moments for the drinks to be served.

"I just came into an inheritance," he said. "I'm trying to figure out if I want to invest in a business, or just buy a great piece of property."

Now she was getting somewhere. "I can understand the frustration of not knowing what to do."

He smiled at her. "Yeah, I guess you could identify." He took the shot of tequila and extracted the residue off his mustache with his lower lip. "Before the inheritance I was in excavation work. Digging, blasting, using all the big equipment."

Bingo. While she leaned forward to get a gulp of her cola, someone tapped on her shoulder. So engrossed by what Ryan just said, until that moment she was unaware anyone else was in the room.

She jumped slightly when she saw Stanton and then jerked at the hem of her skirt to cover her legs. She suddenly felt guilty, but for the life of her she couldn't understand why.

Taking a deep breath she said, "Stanton. Uh...this is Ryan Allan."

Ryan stood up and started to reach out a hand in greeting, but stepped back when Stanton pulled Maya onto the dance floor.

Stanton's timing couldn't have been worse. She'd almost gained all the information she needed. Now she'd have to start the miserable process again with an explanation of why she was whisked away by another man. She tried to turn to look at Ryan, but Stanton held her firm.

Slow dancers were moving around them and Stanton put her arms around his neck, but kept her back far enough so he could see her face when she talked. Looking at his face at close range, his lips in particular, made it darn hard to keep her mind on her mission, but she was determined.

"Why'd you do that? That was rude. We were having a discussion and you interrupted it."

His only answer was a frown. She started to pull away and he tightened his grip. "Answer some questions, first."

"Why is it I have to answer questions, but you don't, Mr. Private Life."

"We'll discuss me later."

"Yeah, right. The only thing I'll learn about you is what's on the back flap of your books."

He gave her a warning glare. "How long have you known this man?"

She looked up at the clock. "Maybe twenty minutes."

"You were letting him pick you up."

"Maybe."

"That's not a safe thing to do."

"I'm safe. Don't you see? Lots of people around."

He sighed. "I didn't think you were that kind of girl."

She smirked. "What kind of girl is that?"

"I think you know what I'm talking about."

"Like I don't have needs?" Maya asked.

They were dancing, slightly, but he leaned her back to assess her face. "You're not talking about what I think you're talking about, are you?"

Looking at him, she frowned, thinking he could stand here and guess all night if he wanted to. She didn't have to answer to him. Then she decided she didn't have time to stand here all night. She had other plans. With Ryan. However, she still didn't know what to ask Ryan without revealing she was doing a little private eye work. Turning, she put a kink in her neck trying to look back at him.

"Relax, Valentine."

Hardly. She wondered if she should make a struggle and try to push him away and then nixed that idea as they already had onlookers. Stanton always had eyes following him. She relaxed her hold.

"That's better," Stanton said.

"Pig," she said in a resigning tone of voice.

"Now, what kind of needs are you talking about?" he asked.

"Same kind of human needs you have. I'm trying to take charge of my life."

"Well, you'd think that after someone just broke into your house, you'd be more careful who you tried to make friends with."

"I am being careful."

"Then why are you dressed like this, Maya?"

"Because I was going out," she said slowly as if she were talking to a special education student. "I thought you were going out of town."

He acted as if he was watching something over her head but then again, he could have been avoiding her question.

"Well?"

"I started writing." He studied her face. "Maya, I'm just concerned about you. Who's here for you, except Alice?"

She didn't want his sympathy. "I don't see Alice here trying to protect me. She happens to think I have a brain in my head."

This was foolishness. Stanton had Michelle, he should not have to worry about her. No, Stanton would not stick around for Maya Valentine, so she needed to start taking charge of her life. Someone was taking gold from her backyard and she would take care of it by herself, starting with Ryan Allan.

Maya hoped for a fast paced song so they could get off the dance floor. She was not so lucky. A slow, very romantic song from Garth Brooks filled the room.

"I think you're smart, too. Beautiful and sexy," he said softly in her ear. "You're strong, but you also can be vulnerable." He drew her closer, and the closeness and compliments made her lightheaded. She sighed and melted into him. He kissed her neck briefly.

Maybe, she thought, just maybe he didn't want to go see Michelle. Maybe he only wanted to be with her. After all, he deemed her desirable. More than ever, she was glad she wore this dress and looked her best.

She looked up into Stanton's eyes. They were intent dark embers, smoldering with what looked like desire. She had no doubt that at this moment he wanted her.

She laid her head on his shoulder, smelled his aftershave and then sighed peacefully.

Maya thought about nibbling his neck just before the music stopped. But he pulled her rather abruptly to the entrance of Princess Pat's, then out the door and into the parking lot.

"You're going home," he said.

With the cool air came the stark reality that perhaps he wasn't feeling the same things she'd been feeling on the dance floor. His attitude was more like big brother coming to take little sister home.

She was mad enough to spit, but stopped after only one pucker. "What am I to you? That you can tease me on the dance floor one minute, then callously send me home the next?"

"Well, you've done something similar to me."

She supposed she couldn't argue with that. She crossed her arms. "I'm not going home yet." Closing her eyes, she dismissed him, then turned to go back into the bar.

Unmindful of her skirt, he threw her over his shoulder and headed to her car. "Hey! Hey!"

He dumped her into her car seat.

The hem of her dress had moved up to where her thighs came together and she watched his eyes linger there. "I dare you to finish what you started on the dance floor," she said through clenched teeth.

Several emotions crossed his face before he shut her car door and walked away.

CHAPTER TEN

*M*aya tripped over Wonder Dog when she dashed to her cell phone. She straightened herself, then on the fifth ring she answered a little breathlessly. Breathless partly from the commotion and partly because she hoped it was Stanton calling to ask for heartfelt forgiveness.

It was only Eve wanting to know if she was ready to sell yet. She was so surprised that it took a moment for her to collect her thoughts.

"I said, are you ready to draw up papers yet? On the house."

Maya was irritated, but tried not to show it, realizing until her problems ceased Eve could still be valuable. Finally, she said, "I met Ryan Allan last night."

"I beg your pardon."

"You know, Ryan Allan, the man who is interested in my house."

Eve was quiet for a moment, then cleared her throat and said, "I'm sorry, I don't know who that is."

"Remember you told me about a man who inherited some money and he was interested in property out in the country?"

"I was referring to someone else. I don't know this Ryan–Allan did you say?"

Maya felt her spirits plummet. If Ryan wasn't the guy and she was sure he was, then what other resource did she have to find this man?

"You're sure?"

"Of course I'm sure. Did you want this Ryan to buy your property?"

"No. No." She tried to think what else she could do besides put her house up for sale to find out who this other man was.

"Give me just a little more time, Eve. My neighbor, Alice Roberts, has been quite ill and I'd like to make sure she's feeling better before I move. So you see, I have a lot on my mind right now. Just a little more time," she said, finishing the call.

Wonder Dog was in her way again as she made her way to the coffee pot. "It's fortunate I didn't stay and play with Ryan Allan," she said to Wonder and he thumped his tail.

She shuddered. She realized now she'd been stupid to try to get Ryan's attention when she didn't know him from Adam, and all she knew about Chad was where he worked. She put her hands on her face and groaned. What could have happened if Stanton hadn't intervened? Still, she wasn't about to thank Stanton, especially when he took her out of Princess Pat's caveman style.

Wonder Dog followed Maya along the dusty gravel road up to Alice's house. Feeling the sun's heat on her back she slowed her pace while Wonder Dog, tongue nearly dragging, went ahead and waited for her at Alice's door.

Alice told her she'd spent the last two hours discussing the area's history with Stanton. She had a little gleam in her eye and Maya envied this moment of euphoria he'd given Alice.

She mentally shook her head, trying to focus on what Alice tried to tell her between coughs.

"Before he leaves, he wants me to go over some of his work," Alice said proudly.

The thought of Stanton leaving made her heart plummet. A cloud of disappointment came over her even though she knew it would be the best thing. She wondered precisely when she could start to get her life back to normal. "When will he be leaving Salisbury Junction?"

"Oh, not any sooner than the end of summer, he said."

Maya sighed. She would have no time this summer without him, unless he was through using her for a tour guide.

"Alice? Since he's coming to see you now to find out what he needs to know, then he won't be needing my services anymore will he?"

"I asked him that and he said he still planned to use you. Lucky girl."

"That's not my definition of lucky. Lucky's like winning the lottery, not spending an afternoon arguing with Stanton."

"That makes my point, my dear. Why would he want to spend an afternoon with you when the little sparks fly? I think it's for no other reason than he's attracted to you. There's not another place he can't visit alone, so why else would he be persistent about seeing you?"

She thought little sparks hardly defined their problems. "To torture me?"

"Again I say, lucky girl."

Maya sniffed, then turned from Alice. She wasn't mad at Alice. Quite the contrary, she only wished she could have Alice's light, easy-going attitude about Stanton.

Alice's coughing or laughing, she couldn't tell which, drove Maya to quickly put the woman's house in order, so she could be on her way. Keeping busy would also put Stanton out of her mind. She had plenty of other things to think of besides him.

Maya did some vacuuming, washed the dishes in the sink and mopped the kitchen floor. When she finished the chores, she looked at the clock, then to Alice. "Tell me about the other bordering neighbors, Alice."

"Well, Patsy and Jim Morris, they live behind both of us. They are about as old as I am. Don't get out much, I understand. You remember Patsy, don't you, dear? When you were younger, I think you must have met her."

She thought hard. Perhaps she had. She wasn't sure. "Any children?"

"They had a son. He drowned when he was not more than ten."

Now she remembered. At least she remembered hearing that horrible story.

"Bureau of Land Management on the other side of you–towards the back part of your property behind the Johnson place. You're wanting to know your borders, does that mean you're thinking of selling?" Alice fooled with the top button of her duster.

Maya took a moment to answer. She didn't want Alice to learn the real reason she wanted to know about the property lines. Alice barely had enough energy to worry about history let alone Maya's troubles. "I don't know, Alice."

She noticed Alice's eyes were clouding up when she said, "I don't want you to go, Maya. I feel bad about bothering you with my problems when you need some peaceful time here in the area. Please don't think I'll always be a burden to you, dear. I promise to be a better neighbor. Although I'll never be a good enough neighbor to repay you for what you do for me. You've taken care of me and you've helped keep Stanton here."

Maya felt like crying and left before Alice could see it. She wouldn't think about saying goodbye to her now. She wondered how she could possibly move away from this woman. This woman who loved her.

After fighting back tears she focused on her problems at hand and wondered on her journey home if the BLM would be stupid enough to be blasting more than a little off their map. She'd make a call or two. Then she would make another trip out on her property and look for more clues. Something must be there, something that could leave some trace, tracks or evidence.

She certainly hoped it would be as easy as a Bureau mistake.

BOOMER HAD A MEETING WITH EVE DOLE. HE HAD TO SEE HER A LITTLE more often than he previously thought and it made real estate a whole lot more interesting.

To her credit, she was very professional. She seemed the type to get out there and get what she desired. Yes, just the type of personality he wanted in a woman.

Except, now Eve told him that Ms. Valentine was not in a hurry to sell, that they needed to back off for a while. Maya Valentine had a sick neighbor to tend. It may take some time before she would sell.

Well, the old woman was sick, that's why Maya spent so much time at her home. He'd also learned in town that this woman, this Alice Roberts, was teaching Stanton Black the area's history. His end was near anyway. What mattered was that Maya would sell. Sell soon. To make that possible, Alice Roberts would have a visitor.

WONDER DOG CHASED THE ATV ABOUT TWO HUNDRED FEET THEN turned back toward the house. Maya was alone now but undeterred with her trusty cell phone in case of an emergency. The problem was she had to climb a hill to get reception.

That's just what she did. She shut off the ATV, climbed up a hill and looked down to the area where the vandalism occurred. Seeing movement, she stepped back and sat at the side of the hill. Flattening herself against the ground, she crawled to the edge of the hillside.

She spotted an ATV loaded with supplies. Then she saw him, a tall, older man with a few days growth of whiskers and salt and pepper hair, unkempt around his shoulders. Black T-shirt and worn jeans. He reminded her a lot of Willie Nelson, except this man limped.

She tried to call the police on her cell phone, but it was out of range of service. She had to climb higher and that was going to be hard to do crawling on her belly like a lizard.

Her heart sped up when he looked her way, then to her right, as if he were feeling eyes on him. Ducking down, she couldn't have been any closer to the earth unless she was buried in it. She stayed like that until she heard the ATV start and move away. Slowly she sat up and caught sight of him leaving across BLM land.

Oh, no! It was too late to call the police now.

When her heart settled, she made her way over to where he had parked his ATV and looked around the area for clues. She found a pile of boulders and diggings, evidence he worked where the earth had been blasted away.

All that was left behind was a paper cup that hadn't burned in the campfire. She carefully picked it up by the bottom rim, with a tissue she had in her pocket, and took it with her hoping fingerprints would show up.

What should she have done. Made her presence known? Perhaps told him he was on her property? No, her instinct told her to stay back. She figured it was better to be safe than sorry.

The sheriff could take care of it now that he had a description and some fingerprints. Now maybe her problems were over. She was optimistic until Sheriff Crawford's laughter came through her cell.

"Fingerprints on a cup, Miss Valentine? Do you think that's enough to go on?" he asked. "I told you to make yourself known. Talk to your neighbors, they probably know all about it."

"But what about the fingerprints?"

"You probably put yours right over his."

"What is your part in this, Mr. Crawford?" she asked, frustrated.

"Okay, I can check the prints. If I find something useable who's to say that his fingerprints are registered anywhere. I'll also make a record of this call. You talk to your neighbors, young lady."

She pushed the screen's stop button before she told him what he should do and it wouldn't have been in the bohemian language either. But to Sam's credit, he did have a point with the fingerprints.

While staring at the clock and tapping her fingernails on the table, she came up with an idea. She'd do a little tavern hopping tonight. A little dinner here, a little dessert there. She would find some old miners and see if she could find out who this man was. It was better than sitting at home and doing nothing.

She thought of Stanton and knew he'd have a fit if he knew her plans. But this was her business not his, and she would be careful–no dressing up as she did the other night at Princess Pat's. In fact, she'd wear plain old jeans and no makeup. She knew better than to leave with anyone and she had her cell phone in case of emergency.

Boy, what she wouldn't give for a girlfriend to go with her.

HER FIRST COURSE OF DINNER CAME AT SEVEN O'CLOCK AT A LITTLE tavern at the edge of town. The place was old, but she couldn't really say dirty because the light was too dim to tell. However, the candle-light from a table did expose water stains of different degrees from the windows down the wall. It reeked of old and new cigarette smoke.

At the bar, she ordered half a deli-style sandwich since the place didn't give her an appetite for anything else.

She looked at her sandwich, then at the bartender who smiled in return. What, she wondered, was she supposed to say? The bartender saved her the trouble. "What's a woman like you doing in a place like this?"

She chuckled and propped her head up with an elbow and fist. "I'm looking for miners."

At around fifty or so, he was tall and quite thin. "Is that singular or plural?" he asked and then poured a hard drink for the man in the back corner.

He left the bar before she got a chance to answer and her gaze followed him while he set the drink before the only other customer.

"Thanks, Bill."

"You're welcome, but that's the last drink you're getting here tonight. You got anybody to take you home?"

"No, but maybe some of my buds will pop in."

"Hope so."

Maya followed the bartender with the turn of her bar stool. "Bar-tender Bill, is it?"

"Yes, ma'am."

"Do miners ever get together and share stories? You know, like what they've found."

"Sure, sometimes. At least this time of year when the weather's good enough to do some searching."

Good, she thought, perhaps she had the right idea. "Here? Do they come here?"

"Excuse me, but somehow I feel like I'm on a hidden camera or something. A pretty girl coming in here and asking for miners."

She laughed, but he didn't. "I'm a big city girl with an interest in mining history, that's all."

"I know some history," he said, then wiped the counter in front of him with a white towel. "My dad used to work in the mines. Do you want to know about one of the big mines?"

She looked down at her sandwich but still didn't take a bite. Two more men came in, gave her the once-over, and then greeted Bill.

"What's up?" One of them asked, then kicked the foot of the other patron in the room. He straightened from his stupor, but didn't appear to visually connect with the two men. One took a seat at the table next to the man and the other took a stool at the bar next to her.

"Tony needs a ride home tonight."

"What else is new?" He looked at Bill, then at Maya. "My name's Ed."

"Hello, I'm Stella," she lied, then took a bite of sandwich.

"Funny, you don't look like a Stella. I haven't seen you around. New in town?"

"I'm passing through."

"She has an interest in mining history," said Bill.

"Well, you've come to the right guy. Bill knows the history. Give me a Bud Light and tell us all about it, Bill."

"Coming up."

Maya watched the Bud Light foam over the top of the glass and onto the counter. "Actually Bill, I'd like to get in on some mining discussions," she said, then resented saying something that sounded that stupid. Especially when both men looked at her, jaws slack, eyebrows raised.

"You need to join a mining group," said Ed. "There's a couple around that meet every so often."

"Like a club you mean." She sat up taller.

"Yep," Ed partially said and partially slurped. "I'd be very happy to take you. That is, I don't see any rings, so I assume you're single."

"Actually, I'm engaged," she said, not wanting to lead him on in any

117

way. "Tell me where and when?"

"I think one meets once a month, right Bill?"

"Yep, it met two days ago."

Maya slumped again. A month was too long to wait.

"If you're engaged, why are you here alone?" Ed asked, visually sweeping her body.

"He's meeting me shortly," she lied again. Ed took it for truth and took his beer over to where his two friends sat, leaving her alone with Bill the bartender.

"It might be better for you if you had your fiancé do the asking in a bar, ma'am."

Why did everyone want to protect her? She looked at her sandwich again. It irked her, yet she knew that if she turned toward Ed again and made conversation, he'd be back at her like a fly stuck on flypaper. It wasn't fair. She decided to cut to the chase and ask about her mystery man.

"Bill? Do you know of a man who's a miner in the area, that's tall, medium weight, with salt and pepper hair?"

"That would be half the miners in this area. You have to be more specific."

"He looks like Willie Nelsen and he limps."

Bill rubbed his chin. "Why yes, I think I do."

"You do?" she asked excited. "What's his name? Does he come here often?"

"Yeah, he comes here sometimes. Haven't seen him in a while. I don't recall his name, though. Ed?"

"Yeah, Bill?"

"You know that guy who's got that bad limp? Comes in here sometimes? The lady here's asking about him."

"That's who you're engaged to, Stella? He doesn't look like your type."

She put a hand on her chest and said, "Oh, no. No. My interest in him is strictly to do with mining." She realized that was probably the most truthful statement *Stella* made all evening. She'd have to watch this lying stuff. This was a small town.

Bill cut in, "What was his name? Do you remember?"

"Man, I can't remember either. Sorry, Stella. He's kind of a quiet guy, keeps to himself. Sorry I can't be more help than that."

The cigarette smoke irritated her throat. She looked at her watch. She'd already wasted half an hour. Taking her sandwich, she moved to a table far from Ed's party and tried to finish eating.

A man wearing a cowboy hat walked through the entrance, a circular can of chewing tobacco showing in a back pocket. He took a seat at the bar and ordered a shot of whiskey with a beer chaser.

Three other men stepped in, two with skin calloused hands, and tape measures attached to their belts. She didn't know how to approach these people, nor felt inspired to keep asking dumb, none-of-her-business questions. What she needed was a TV cop where the crime was solved in one hour's time.

When a man grabbed his beer and headed for her table, she decided to make a quick exit. She grabbed her purse and said a farewell and thank you to Bill.

She wouldn't quit her day job to become a detective. She'd go to Princess Pat's. With more women in attendance, she'd feel a little more comfortable and perhaps be in a more normal atmosphere for a game of twenty questions.

At Princess Pat's, she took a bar stool, ordered a piece of Marionberry and peach pie *a la mode*, then looked around. She didn't know a soul and felt lonely in consequence.

A couple of girls sat at a nearby table. One reminded her of her best friend who moved to North Carolina, same shade of blonde hair and long limbs.

Maya sighed, then was pleasantly surprised when she bit down on one of the best desserts she ever tasted. She'd spooned in probably a thousand calories when a waitress asked if she could get her something to drink. Maya asked if she knew of a miner who limped and the woman laughed and said, "Sorry, we don't serve that drink here."

Just then, Ryan Allan walked in the door. It didn't take him more than a moment to catch Maya's welcoming smile. He wasn't the trespasser on her property and she was less fearful of him. She knew he had an interest in mining and believed he'd do just fine in a question and answer game.

"No dress tonight? I'm afraid I miss it."

"Sorry, but maybe some other night, Ryan."

"You remembered my name. I'm honored. I don't see your boyfriend here tonight. Does that mean anything?"

"It means he's not my boyfriend. I believe Michelle Karr is more his style."

"Do you mean that actress? Wow."

She hated hearing how wonderful Michelle was, but tried not to show her discomfort. She needed a quick change of subject and what better topic than her current mission. "Ryan, do you belong to a mining group? I mean, I remember you said you were here for the gold."

"Actually, yeah." He stopped to order a beer. "Um, yeah. A couple of groups get together around here. Are you interested in going to one of them?"

"I might, yes."

"Well, then maybe I could take you. Huh?"

She didn't want to answer just yet. "Do many miners attend these meetings?"

He nodded. "Yes, one of them. Pretty good crowd for Salisbury Junction, I guess."

Maya looked out across the faces of the tavern's patrons, trying to form the right words to get the information she was after. She wished she could be truthful and flat out ask about the intruder on her property. Nevertheless, she hardly knew this man and for all she knew he could be conspiring with the perpetrator. After all, he told her that he was in this area for the gold mining.

"They talked about one of the old mines the last time we met," he said.

"Sounds interesting." She meant it. Perhaps the area's allure rubbed off on her after all.

"It was the Virtue Mine."

She was thinking she hadn't heard of that one when she spotted Ed from the previous tavern coming in. He motioned with his hand for someone to follow. Ed located her at once and pointed in her direction.

She gasped when his friend stepped in. "Oh, no!" He was the man with the limp.

Ryan looked over his shoulder. "Something wrong?"

"No."

The man's eyes focused on her and he frowned.

A shiver of fear ran through her. "Excuse me, I'm going to the restroom."

Inside she stood behind the door, heart racing while waiting for the man to force his way in. She locked the latch on the stall door. Of all the rotten luck, to have Ed tell him she was looking for him. She couldn't confront him on her own.

Her instincts told her she shouldn't involve Ryan. It was a small town and both men were interested in mining. They could be friends as far as she knew. No, she wouldn't involve Ryan in this.

Sitting on the toilet seat, she grabbed her purse to her chest. That's when she remembered her cell phone. Biting her bottom lip until she could taste blood, she contemplated whether she should call the sheriff or not. She knew what Sam Crawford would say.

He would expect her to introduce herself and then calmly tell him he had been trespassing on her property. This man had a hard look to his face, so much so that he looked scary. She highly doubted he'd be neighborly about the whole situation.

She fumbled nervously with her purse until she pulled out her cell phone. If not the police, then whom should she call? She wished she knew someone to call.

The only one she could call was Stanton. She pressed in Alice's number and asked her as sweetly as she could what for Charles Johnson phone number.

"Have you been running, dear?" Alice asked.

"No, I go to go. Bye."

Her heart picked up a few more beats when he pushed in the number. "Please answer, Stanton. Please answer."

She bent down and tried to look across the neighboring stalls. She didn't see any other feet. So much for safety in numbers.

What if he came in? What in the world would she say to him? That she thought he was cute and she wanted to meet him? She didn't think that would work, especially if he knew who she was and where she lived.

"Stanton," she nearly screamed, then made an effort to be quiet.

"Maya, is that you?"

"Yes," she said with a gasp when someone entered the restroom. She carefully looked down and over without exposing herself. She saw a woman's shoes and let out a breath.

"Are you all right?" Stanton asked.

She lowered her voice to a whisper. "No, not very good. Could you come pick me up?"

"Where are you? What's wrong? I can barely hear you, Maya."

"I'm at Princess Pat's. I need you to come here."

"Did your car break down?" She noted a touch of skepticism in his voice.

"Just a minute." Maya thought she heard another noise. She realized it was only the woman leaving the neighboring stall. After hearing the water turn on and off, she heard the door open and close. She pulled her knees up and managed to put her feet on the seat so that she'd be hidden.

She felt comfortable enough to let her voice rise from a whisper. "My car's fine. I'm just here by myself." She didn't quite know how to explain this to Stanton. "A guy is looking for me and I'm hiding in the restroom."

"Well, Valentine, isn't that why you went in the first place? For a guy, I mean."

She sighed. He obviously didn't see how desperate she was. "That's not true, at least not the way you're thinking."

The restroom door opened and she pulled her knees in tighter.

"Stella!" It took her only a moment to recognize the name she'd given Ed.

"What was that?" Stanton asked. "Sounds like, what was the name of that movie? Oh, *A Streetcar Named Desire*. Stella!" Stanton mimicked.

"That's who he thinks I am," she whispered.

"Why did you give him a false name?"

"I'm serious, Stanton, I'm scared," she whispered the best she could.

Stanton was silent for a moment, all she heard was the pounding of her heart and the occasional squeak of the restroom door.

"Tell him you'll be out in a minute or two. That you're not feeling good." Then he was gone, she heard dial tone.

She put her feet down to make it look as if she were using the toilet. She said, "I'll be out in a minute or two. I'm not feeling too good." Then she held her breath and gritted her teeth until she heard the door close.

Time went by slower than she'd ever remembered while she sat waiting. She hoped that Ed was drinking himself into oblivion by now and forgetting all about her.

He hadn't. In five minutes, he was back looking for "Stella."

"Just give me five more minutes, okay? I'm sure I'll feel better by then. Something's just not agreeing with me."

"Okay," Ed answered slowly.

In five more minutes, she knew Stanton would be there and her troubles would be over. She calmed down long enough to realize she'd be going from one madness to another since she was sure Stanton would be angry. If she disturbed his writing, she was going to pay for it.

"S-t-e-l-l-a!" It was Stanton this time doing his best impression of Marlon Brando.

Maya rushed out of her stall into the doorway and threw her arms around his neck. He returned her hug, but at the same time walked her back into the restroom. The door swung shut behind them.

"Who is it, Maya?"

"It's two guys, actually. One's named Ed and I don't know the name of the other. What should we do?" They moved aside while a woman made an attempt to enter.

"I've got a plan. Let's go. If I get my fingers broken, you're going to pay, Valentine."

She faltered. She hadn't thought of any danger to Stanton. Hurting his hands would stop his writing career for a while.

"Come on. It's now or never. This lady wants privacy, I'm sure."

He got a good grip on her arm and began pulling her across the tavern toward the door. She tried to keep his pace.

"Stella," Ed called out, meeting them as they were nearly to the door.

"So Stella it is today, darlin'? I'm sorry, sir, but she does this nearly every week. Hittin' the bars looking for men, then ends up cowerin' in the bathroom. Actually, I'm gettin' tired of this wild goose chase and I'll be seeking some professional help for ol' Stella here."

Ed was obviously dumbfounded, standing with his mouth ajar. Maya turned her head, quickly scanning the room for the man with the limp. He was not in the room. She saw Ryan standing by the bar where she left him, no doubt scowling at her because she was leaving with the same man he'd seen her leave with before. She was sorry for that.

"No, come on Stella, no more men tonight." He gave her arm a final tug and she stumbled out the door.

"Stanton! Why did you say that? This is a small town in case you hadn't noticed."

"I prevented a fight."

"You lied. I was looking for a man, yes, but not like you said."

"Case in point. You were looking for a man and you were last week, too. To your credit, you were only barricaded in the bathroom one of the times, so far. Professional help is up to you."

"Oh!" She stopped and crossed her arms against her chest. Turning from him she stomped her foot in anger. At this angle she saw the man with the limp make the corner of the building on foot. It didn't take her long to realize he'd been watching them.

"That's him," she exclaimed and positioned herself behind Stanton.

"Yeah, well he's gone now. We're better off just getting in our cars and going home, Maya."

"I can't go home, Stanton. He'll find me there."

"He knows your address? It wasn't very smart to give a stranger your address. Didn't you say you were from a big town?"

She stood dumbfounded, looking at the spot where the man had last been.

"Come on. You've got some 'splainin' to do, Lucy." He helped her into his pickup, a frown knit on his brow. He got in and despite the steering wheel, turned his whole body toward her. "What's your problem, Maya? What's all this?"

Her problem? All of a sudden it struck her that she was here this summer trying to relax from the busy school year. Perhaps even enjoy herself by trying to remember her late father and hopefully relive some of the wonderful memories of her childhood vacations. Even see if it was possible for her to love this area as much as he had, to somehow make it feasible to keep the property for many years to come.

She hardly had a moment to meditate on any of this, since immediately on her arrival she dealt with Alice's illness and Stanton's need of her as a tour guide. Not to mention her property and home vandalized. Then she remembered her underwear spread out across her bed and she shuddered with a gripping fear.

Stanton cleared his throat, signaling her to answer and she wondered how much to tell him. Besides his curiosity about her predicament tonight, she believed he wouldn't want to be involved in any of this. She didn't really want that, anyway. She'd take care of her own problems, some way, somehow.

"Thank you so much for coming to my aid tonight, Stanton. I won't do it again."

After a moment, he said, "That's it? No explanation?"

She put a hand on his arm tenderly. "Just thank you. It was good of you to come help me."

"Help me, what?"

"Get out safely," she said, attempting to sound matter of fact.

STANTON REALIZED HE REALLY DID HAVE SOME FEELINGS FOR HER. HIS reaction to her phone call had made him break into a sweat and break the speed limit, if not the sound barrier, in his attempt to get to Princess Pat's in time. He felt great relief when he found out she was okay. Just to look in the restroom and see her feet sticking out of the stall did his heart good.

Then came anger that she duped him into getting there under false pretenses. False pretenses due to the fact it looked like nonsense. If he were to write this little episode in a book, his fans would never believe it.

For the life of him, he couldn't figure out what she wanted. He'd spent a lot of time trying to reason this all out. He even resorted to following her one evening and turned up at Princess Pat's, luckily before she could do any damage to herself. Now here he was again.

Every time he thought he'd figured her out, she proved him wrong. She didn't want his money. She seemed to find him attractive, yet he was not on her list of dateable males. Even if he made the list, nothing was long-term about the two of them since he was sure she was only in this part of the country temporarily.

Yet, she wanted him here again at Princess Pat's. Why? Because she needed someone to protect her? Most people would have just called the police. Not Maya. She wanted an author to help her. Made lots of sense to him.

MAYA HAD HER OWN THOUGHTS. SHE STARTED TO CALM DOWN, NOW better able to think. She'd stay at Alice's tonight, that's what she'd do. She'd think of some excuse so she wouldn't worry.

Then tomorrow, she'd go into town and try to work something out with Sam Crawford. If he wouldn't listen, she'd find someone else who would. She felt better now that she had a plan. She also wondered if Salisbury Junction was large enough to have a private investigator. She highly doubted it.

She took a deep breath. "I feel better. I'll just go to my own car now," she said.

He put his arm out to block her. "Well, I don't feel better. You're the most unpredictable woman I have ever met, you know that, Maya? And frankly your behavior of late has been frightening."

Maya didn't take the comment too personally since she knew he wouldn't think that if he'd known what she'd been going through.

"I can understand your irritation, Stanton, after all I probably interrupted your writing. I have to go to the bathroom."

He withdrew his arm and leaned back. She could see the muscle clenching in his jaw signaling his vexation. She leaned back and positioned her elbow on the door's armrest while she waited for the verbal onslaught of his fury.

"You have to go to the bathroom? You've just been in the bathroom for who knows how long and now you have to go to the bathroom?"

"Well, have some sympathy, will ya? I've had a rough night," she said, her voice rising.

"If you go out blatantly looking for more male attention, then you best not turn around and be a tease about it. How can you not expect trouble otherwise?"

"What? I'm not a tease." She was outraged at the thought.

"From your actions tonight, I say otherwise," he said with a new calmness. What looked like pity in his eyes dispelled any anger she felt. He had believed she was something she wasn't and he pitied her for it.

"You know if you have to have male attention—and I've heard about women who can't live without a man, you really should go about it in a safer way. Like maybe a church singles group or something."

The man was being ludicrous. She shook her head and looked out the window. *Yeah, The First Church of Miners*, she thought.

"The man I want can't be found in a church."

"Excuse me?"

She'd said too much already. She sighed and looked toward her car.

"So you're not a tease."

Maya looked at him then. "Please, Stanton, I'm not such a mystery. I'm not a tease. I can live without a man and I have to go to the bathroom."

He reached out, grabbed her under her arms and pulled her partially onto his lap. The steering wheel cut at her back.

"Well, Miss Game Player, then that means you just want a physical relationship. I suppose I can help you with that. That is what you want, right? Just me and you and a simple physical relationship?"

Her jaw dropped and her eyes narrowed. "You're thinking I put you up to this, so I could get–close to you?"

He nodded. "That's the only thing that makes sense to me."

She couldn't believe her ears. "And the world revolves around you–"

He put his hands on her face and cut off her words with a kiss. A gentle kiss, his lips warm and soft. She found herself momentarily thinking Jeff's lips were never this conductive to sensual gratification. Stanton's tongue was sweet and wet; she took it in and savored it until he broke the kiss to move his lips to her throat.

She buried her face in his hair, taking in the scent and softness of it and melting into him. Her former desire to lick his face now came into being when she put her lips on his face and tasted his skin again and again.

He took in a sharp intake of breath and then a moan. Without a doubt, he was the most carnal male she'd ever come across. She loved the sexy look of him and the way his eyes darkened and fastened on her made her believe he longed for her more than any other.

His hand gently patted her stomach. She knew he was in limbo as to whether he should move it up or down.

"Your gypsy spell is working, 'cause I want you real bad."

She jerked back and hit the horn. How sobering the horn was, for both of them. He pushed her back into her seat and rubbed his face with his hands.

"Listen, I don't think we should do this. This is all so crazy," he said. "I guess I'm the tease this time."

It was as though she had an angel on one shoulder and the devil on the other. One tried to convince her to fight to have Stanton in every way possible while the other pointed out how she'd been hurt by a fiancé who left her for another woman. The angel won.

"Maybe so, but you also show some integrity."

His eyes narrowed. "No. It has nothing to do with anything besides the fact that you're a fly-by-night. I'm planning to have a home here. You're not staying. You have a teaching job in Portland. You'll be gone when the summer's over." He shifted in his seat, she assumed for comfort. Then he sighed long and loud. Reaching over her to open the door, he said, "Good night, Valentine."

Maya shut her car door and locked it. She experienced a multitude of feelings with sexual frustration high on the list. And embarrassment. And anger for her stupidity that came out in many ways this night. Still, she was not going to cry.

First Eve, then Alice thought she was thinking of moving, and now Stanton. She fought the lump forming in her throat and it turned into a frustrated ball in her chest. It disturbed and angered her that she couldn't find her own answers. Why was it everyone knew what she was going to do except herself?

Her former plans of going to Alice's for the night canceled, her anger now driving her home. She hit the steering wheel with her fist. "Just try to come after me tonight, Mr. Miner, and I'll beat you to a bloody pulp with my bare hands," she shouted.

BOOMER TOOK A GULP OF BEER AND CLAPPED HIS MUG ON THE TABLE. He swore. Maya seemed to know who he was. She could give his description to the police. Well, he'd have to get closer to the woman than he'd wanted.

However, when he'd seen the edge of fear on her face when she'd looked at him, he was glad of the bit of power he now had over her. For where there was fear there was power. He'd watch her like a hawk now.

CHAPTER ELEVEN

"*N*o. No, Ms. Valentine, you don't need to take this to someone else in the police department. All right, I'll meet you out at your place and take a look at this cave," said Sam Crawford.

Maya sighed. "Okay."

"Give me a little time to find a legal property description and a map of the place to check your borders."

What? She wanted this settled ASAP! Frustrated, she tapped her foot on the floor, wondering what to say next. She supposed it wouldn't do her any good to tell him she knew where the markers were. Somehow, she'd have to be patient just a little while longer.

"Fine. I think the side the Bureau of Land Management owns would be the best way to get through to the back of my property. I'll meet you out there."

When she'd told Sam about the man with the limp it sounded like a tall tale even to her own ears. But, someone had broken into her house and she had no definite proof that this incident connected to the vandalism on the back of her property. Her gut feeling told her it all tied together and knew she could get hurt trying to separate a man from his gold.

It was almost unthinkable that her lack of sleep last night had a lot to do with Stanton Black. She couldn't figure out how he could possibly know the outcome of her summer vacation when she hadn't a clue. He was so sure.

Through the night her mind took her back to the way lust shot through her, from her head to her toes and settled in her middle when he touched her. Over and over she only envisioned those moments, not the trouble that happened before or after their coming together.

Reality came with the morning light.

Her sigh came from deep within her soul. She felt tired and weary, not only from lack of sleep but from struggling and suffering to fight the attraction she felt for Stanton while trying to do the right thing.

Soon Alice would heal and then Stanton wouldn't complicate her life any longer.

As she sped away on the ATV, Wonder Dog started to follow her, then turned back to the comforts of home. She was alone now and realized she'd forgotten her cell phone. She didn't think it mattered because she was meeting Sam in a few minutes and hopefully he'd settle all this. Then she could go down to the water's edge with a good book and try to really enjoy what might be her last summer here.

Maya could see how illogical it would be to sell the place. She felt terrible even considering selling because it belonged to her family and it hurt to think of other people living where she'd lived so happily with her parents. This was the only place in the world where she had known any security and she had such tender feelings for the land. It seemed she was familiar with every tree, every stone. Now she wished she would have buried her father here or at least in a nearby graveyard.

It was hard losing her mother, but she had her father to help her through it. She at least had one parent left. Now alone, it seemed ten times harder grieving for her father. He seemed to be right here in the woods, at the river and sometimes even at the house. Her father's spirit seemed to live there, as well as the spirit of her dear mother. She wondered what he'd think about her being in Salisbury Junction.

Heading up a slight incline, Maya's mind went back to when her father first purchased the ATV. He'd talked about buying one for some time, checking the newspaper ads for a good buy. When he'd found just the right rig, he was like a child with a new toy. He told her once he'd traveled over every inch of his beloved property.

The sentimental value was here all right, but what would she do with all this acreage? Would a bigger town be a better place for a single woman looking for friends and perhaps a husband one day? Somehow, she'd have to make a decision soon.

She thought she'd better focus on the task at hand and at least appear mentally balanced to Mr. Crawford. With the sheriff in mind, she drove right down close to the cave.

She'd forgotten to bring a flashlight. She searched through a zippered pouch attached to the ATV and found some matches.

After two unsuccessful tries, she lit the match. The first thing she spotted once inside the mouth of the cave was an air compressor. Some hoses, various tools and equipment lay about.

The match was about to burn her fingers, so she shook it out. She grew panicky in the darkness until she managed to light another match. Something shiny caught her eye. On closer examination, she saw a golden jagged streak towards the back wall, running about three feet before it disappeared. She believed it was gold. Obviously someone else did, too.

She stepped out of the cave and looked toward Bureau land. When Sam Crawford didn't appear she looked around and realized how alone she was and it worried her. If someone could build this cave, then that someone could dig a real nice grave and she'd not be heard from again. Even though she hoped Stanton would miss her and look for her. She knew Alice would. The last place they would look for her would be back here.

For a while now, she believed she was in danger. It would be hard for her to live with herself if someone else got hurt because of her. Since she wanted to protect Alice and even Stanton, she had no one to blame but herself for not sharing her present predicament.

A noise caused her to catch her breath. It was only a twig blowing in the wind. When a pinecone fell behind her she jumped. About the time she was ready to high tail it off on the ATV, she heard someone coming. At least that's what it sounded like. She quickly stepped inside the cave and then cautiously tried to look out the entrance. From her position, she couldn't see who approached, and her heartbeat was drowning out the sound of the footsteps.

"Who is it?" she heard a man ask.

She hesitated. Was it Sam's voice?

"I have a gun," he warned.

No, if it were Sam he'd say he was the police. She reached behind to grab a blunt instrument. It was some kind of mallet.

She felt like she was playing a rock-paper-scissors game and came up lacking. She was going to die back here, just like that. Her kin's bad karma seemed to match that of the Kennedy family.

With both hands, she positioned her weapon over her head and waited for the man to get closer. Maybe she could knock the gun out of his hand. She'd pick it up. No, she'd kick it and run. No, then he'd have a chance to grab her. She'd just run. He was probably faster, so she'd pick up the gun and what, shoot him? Could she do it, actually kill someone?

When something hit the entrance of the cave she squealed. It was a rock and it barely missed her.

"Maya? Is that you, Maya Valentine?"

It was Sam, after all. She took a deep breath and worked at calming her heart rate. He'd nearly scared her to death. What was the matter with him, anyway?

"Yes, it's me!" She stepped out of the cave and dropped the mallet. "Whatever happened to 'this is the police, come out with your hands up?'"

"Oh, it's been over-used." He put his gun back in its holster.

"Whew. I'm glad it was you." She knew her heart would calm down eventually.

Sam took a flashlight from his belt and shone it inside the cave. After a few minutes, he turned toward her and refastened his light. "This is no novice," he said. "Look, you can tell because they took the time to arch the entrance. Judging from that streak inside they knew where to find gold."

Maya felt great for the first time in a long time, because now she'd get some help. Her problems were nigh over. Except for Stanton, but she could deal with him now that this was over.

"Thanks so much for coming out here," she said and shook his hand. "I'm very happy this is going to be taken care of."

Sam's eyebrows furrowed and he shook his head. "I don't know what you're thinking ma'am, but we can't afford to post a man out here. Heavens, this character may not be back for a month, for all I know."

"What? You're not going to take care of this?"

He rubbed a hand across his short hair. "I'm sorry, but we can't post a man out here."

"So you came out here for nothing?"

"Well, I wouldn't say for nothing. This will all go into the report."

"Report? What good would that do?"

"If you and your friends sneak out here and video tape him in the act—"

"My friends?" she asked, not believing this conversation was actually taking place. "Well, I'll just get them all together and we'll do that." She dismissed him by walking toward her ATV.

"If you can do that it will work," he shouted after her, obviously missing her sarcasm. "It will go together with the report and we'll have something on him!"

She couldn't ever remember feeling this frustrated. Oh, how she missed her father. She cried for him all the way back to the house.

After putting the ATV away, she wiped the tears from the side of her face with the sleeve of her shirt. The tears had helped relieve her frustration. She stood and looked at the house until she came up with an idea that just might work. She'd list the house and put a for sale sign in the yard come morning.

Maya grabbed a sleeping bag out of the spare bedroom closet. It looked very dusty, but she wasn't about to take anything clean to lie down on next to the river.

At last, she was going to get a chance to rest up and try to think sanely about her future.

She told herself she shouldn't feel so sad. She should count her blessings. She had her health, and thanks to her father and her job she was financially secure. A bonus was having a job in education, giving her lots of vacation time. How many people were that lucky? But she still didn't feel any better.

Now, she hoped a nap would help, and unzipped the sleeping bag, tried to shake the dust off, and then spread it on the ground. She plopped down on her stomach, hidden by bushes and trees, and watched the river flow past. Wonder Dog lay down against her arm for a cozy snooze. Her mind raced and she couldn't sleep.

She thought that if Eve brought this Willie Nelsen look-a-like through the house, she could find out who he was and tell the police. If Eve didn't bring him through, she'd be moving. It might be her only safe choice.

She was fast asleep when a pinprick-like sensation in her arm woke her. Hearing a car going up her drive, she sat up and could see through the trees that the car belonged to Eve. Maya's heart pounded when the man with the limp got out and walked with Eve to the door. When no one answered, Eve used the lock box and let him in.

All she needed to do now was call Eve and get the name of this man and then she could tell the police.

Maya flopped back on the sleeping bag and laughed with glee. Wonder wagged his tail and tried to lick her face. She was so happy she actually let him.

With the incredible relief that her troubles would soon be over, came encouragement to stay in Salisbury Junction. She could be Alice's neighbor and she could help her through her aging years. Alice could help her through her young years. The first thing she was going to do after she talked to Sam was call the Salisbury Junction school district and try and find a teaching job. If not, she could substitute and still make money. Every school needed good substitutes.

She couldn't believe the path her thoughts were taking, but she was glad. No longer trapped into selling her house, she was free.

Not only did she feel happy, she felt smug. She'd tell Stanton that she wasn't moving. Then he'd have to face the music. Now that she was staying, he'd have to fess up about Michelle. He'd have to decide what he really wanted and she could only hope it wasn't just a summer fling.

Eve was not going to be pleased with her. Maya got by this guilt by telling herself that Eve would understand once this man was arrested.

After a time, Eve and her customer left and Maya decided to make her way back to the house. When she bent to pick up the sleeping bag, she noticed that she had a bug bite. Already a slight swelling and faint red marks appeared on the inside of her forearm. It looked like it was going to be one that itched like crazy before it finally healed.

She looked at her watch again and decided to give Eve some time to finish her business, then she'd call and get a name for Sam. Until then, she'd type her letter of resignation and send it off today. She laughed aloud at the fact that she was so happy about being unemployed. Nevertheless, she'd still make some money being a tour guide.

"Yes!" She couldn't wait until tomorrow when she'd see Stanton again. Would he squirm and then stutter about his relationship with Michelle? He would at least have to see that the attraction they had for each other was worth investigating. At the least, it showed that perhaps Michelle wasn't the right one for him. If she was, she doubted he'd be kissing another woman.

This confirmed her emerging thoughts that she was not the right one for Jeff. Where once she thought Jeff was just a cad, she now believed it was not a match made in heaven. She only wished they could have established this fact before he went on to greener pastures.

After typing her resignation, she had no trouble putting it in the mailbox. Looking over at Alice's place she smiled. Alice will be thrilled she was staying.

Upon returning to the house, Maya checked her messages. "Hi, Maya, it's Eve Dole. Guess what? Someone's made an offer on your place! Call me as soon as you get in."

Maya sure hoped it was Willie. She could feel her heart pounding as she waited for Eve to pick up the phone.

"Who is it?" Maya blurted out as Eve introduced herself.

"This must be Maya and I can tell you are just as excited as I am. His name is Charles Johnson," Eve said.

Maya knew the name. It was her neighbor and Stanton's landlord, a man she'd never seen before. She wrote the name on a scrap of paper and said, "Can I call you back?"

"But...but–"

"Goodbye."

The sheriff. Where did she put the sheriff's number? She flipped through her notepad like she was all thumbs but finally found the number.

"Sam Crawford? This is Maya Valentine. We've got him."

"You've got who?"

Did he not remember anything they'd talked about? She bit her tongue for a moment to keep from saying Santa Claus. "The man who's been terrorizing me, that's who. I saw him on my property and again today. I have his name. It's Charles Johnson."

"Well, now that's good. You need to come in and follow procedure."

"Sure, of course."

A nauseous sensation suddenly overwhelmed her and she wondered if the lunch she'd eaten hadn't agreed with her. Her body burned with fever and she felt so listless she knew she'd have to take another nap.

First, she'd call Alice and explain to her why she had a for sale sign on her property.

"You're not selling? Then why do you have a for sale sign up?" After a moment, Alice said, "I said, why do you have a for sale sign on your property if you're not moving? Are you okay, Maya?"

"Actually no, I'm not. I think I'm coming down with something. I may not be over to see you tonight, or tomorrow if I don't feel better. Now what were you saying?"

"Why is there a sign in your yard?"

"I put the house up for sale because I wanted to get the man who was getting gold out of my property. By the way, it's Charles Johnson."

"You're scaring me, Maya. You're not making sense and besides that, Charles Johnson is in Arizona."

Maya decided she'd go over and explain it to Alice when she felt better. She just didn't have the strength right now. "Never mind. I'll tell you later when I can explain. Can you tell me what kind of bugs we have around here? I got a bug bite of some kind down by the river."

"You say down by the river? Are you sure it wasn't just a mosquito?"

"No. It's swelling a bit and it's got some red marks." Her stomach started to cramp and she bent over and moaned.

"Spider bite. Could be a spider bite. They're rarely lethal, just put something cold on it."

Maya doubted she had the energy to do cold packs.

"You don't sound very good. Do you think I should come over and help you through this flu thing?"

"Heavens no. I'm just having the flu with some hard stomach pains. I'll probably feel better after I throw up. You stay away. I don't want you sick. I'll be fine after a bit."

"Well, I'll call you later. You get some rest."

"Thanks, Alice. Alice, I'm not moving. I'm going to be your neighbor forever."

"That's wonderful to hear, dear."

Maya's legs were getting stiff and her back was killing her. Chills had replaced the burning fever. She fetched a quilt and sat on the couch with it. Shooting waves of pain in her back and stomach made her cry out, then she felt like someone was squeezing her arm.

The phone rang, but she didn't pick up. In a few minutes she listened to the message. It was Eve. Evidently, Charles Johnson wanted to make an offer. She was to call back immediately.

Maya didn't think so.

She must have dozed off, for when she heard the phone ring again, it was dark. She could barely move. It was Sam. The message said Charles Johnson was not even in town. He'd talked to him in Arizona. She had named the wrong man.

No. She knew it was Charles Johnson. He was wrong. She'd fix it all later, she thought and turned into the couch to rest. She hurt badly and just needed to rest.

A little later she thought she heard Alice's voice when she touched a button on her phone. She was saying something about appendicitis. What in the heck was that about? She said to pick up the phone. Maya reached toward her cell but the phone dropped as well and for the life of her, she couldn't pick it up.

CHAPTER TWELVE

*S*tanton finally decided how he wanted to work his book and he successfully fleshed the story out. If his luck continued to hold, he'd work through the night as long as this magic would last.

He heard the phone twice. The first was a wrong number and the second was for Charles Johnson. He told whoever it was that Charles was in Arizona and it seemed to placate the caller. Now, nothing else was going to bother him. He took the phone wire from the wall, wrapped it around the phone and then set it on the kitchen table with more force than he should have.

An hour later he realized he was nearly in a trance, since it took a while to grasp the fact that someone kept pounding on his front door. He could feel frustration brewing inside. He was ready to scold the visitor as he opened the door.

For a moment, he stared dumbfounded at Alice Roberts and then opened the glass screen door.

"What are you doing out and about? You can't get well by doing that."

"I'm frightened. Something is really wrong with Maya. Please go and see about her. I don't know where else to turn." She nearly hyperventilated, trying to talk and cough, too.

"Now just sit down and take a deep breath."

She sat and took a deep breath. "Let me explain. Maya called me earlier and she didn't make sense."

Well, what was unusual about that? he wondered. "What did she say?"

"She said that Charles Johnson tried to get gold off her property, so she put the house up for sale."

"That's crazy. Johnson's in Arizona."

"That's what I told her."

"And?"

"She said she'd explain later."

"Did she send you over here? To get me?" He was getting tired of the games, very tired.

"No. No. I came on my own. You see she told me she felt sick, she had bad stomach pains." Alice had to stop to catch her breath. Then she swallowed, and said, "She thought she had the flu. I got worried because, besides what she said about Johnson, she didn't always hear what I was saying. And–and I asked if I should come over and help her out, but she flatly refused."

"No, if she'd gotten the flu then you need to stay away. She'll probably feel better in the morning."

"The thing that frightens me now is that I said I'd call her back tonight and see how she was doing, but she's not answering her phone. I'm real concerned about her."

Stanton doubted that anything was wrong with Maya, but he didn't think Alice would take his word for it. He looked back towards the back bedroom where his work awaited and sighed. Alice needed to get home. He'd just make it quick with Maya.

"You go home. I'll save my work here then go over to see how she's doing."

"Please give me a call when you find out. Oh thank you, Mr. Black."

"Certainly," he said through tight lips.

As usual, Boomer had kept track of Maya. He became comfortable with the sounds of her regular television shows, as well as which lights she utilized.

Except tonight, her usual life's patterns were not in place. Something was amiss. He looked around the house to make sure her car was home and then checked for lights at the back of the house. Finding the house dark, he stepped closer than he'd ever dared before and spotted Maya lying on the floor of the living room.

He'd wondered if she'd committed suicide, and became alarmed. Now he didn't care if she lived or died once she'd turned the property over to him, but if she died first, things could be tied up in court for months. This he could not have. This was not part of his plan. No, it was certainly not.

He cried out an inhuman sound then frantically raced around the house checking and rechecking windows and doors while muttering insanely.

He felt some karmic payback when he found the house sealed as tight as a can of sardines, all due to his vandalism. When he spotted car lights, he tried to calm himself and stepped back into the shadows while waiting to see what fate had in store.

The first thing Stanton saw pulling up the drive was the for sale sign in Maya's yard. He shook his head. Somehow, it hurt that he was right about her. She wouldn't stay.

Everything was dark when he cut the engine but gave the key an extra turn to keep the headlights on, pointing toward the door. He could barely make out a night light in what appeared to be a hallway. He knocked firmly and listened for Maya's dog to bark. All Stanton could hear was the sound of crickets outside.

After he'd knocked a second time, the animal barked like he was a guard dog. Stanton simply figured the dog was hard of hearing. He started to leave when he spotted her car parked on the other side of the house.

Worried, he pounded on the door and then looked in the windows. Something lay crumpled on the floor. It looked like a blanket. When he tried to focus a little harder, he saw it was Maya. Something indeed was wrong and his heart jumped into his throat.

"Maya," he screamed at the top of his lungs. "Get up, Maya!"

She lay as though lifeless.

He thought he was going to have a heart attack the way his heart pounded. He believed Maya dead, and he couldn't bear the thought of her not breathing. It nearly took his own breath away.

He looked around quickly. Of course, she kept the door locked. With her special locks and barred windows, he couldn't get in. Thankfully, he noticed the lock box put in by her realtor. If he had enough time he could get her realtor here and she could open the door.

Grabbing his cell phone, he called the number on the for sale sign and told Eve he would give her a thousand dollars if she could get here on the double with a key to Maya's door.

He then called an ambulance and prayed to God harder than he'd ever prayed in his life.

MAYA DREAMED SOMEONE KNOCKED ON HER DOOR. WONDER DOG barked. Good dog. She didn't need any company. She hurt too badly to have friends. Good thing she didn't have any friends here.

Wonder Dog whined. He probably needed to go to the bathroom. She sat up and slumped onto the floor, doubled up in pain.

"I'm sorry, Wonder Dog," she said. She would just lie where she dropped, get some rest for now and clean up his mess later. She pulled the quilt over her freezing body.

Now light entered the room and someone shook her. She saw her father's dark eyes.

"Daddy." She tried to reach out to him but couldn't.

"You'll be all right," he said and wrapped her tighter in the quilt.

"Daddy, you're here. Oh Daddy, I've missed you so much. I hurt, Daddy." She started to cry.

"Shh!" he said. "It's not your daddy. Shh."

If not him, then who was it? She tried to open her eyes, but couldn't. And it all frightened her. "Willie. Nelsen. Get away, Willie."

He didn't reply.

"No, where are you taking me? No, Willie. No." She couldn't struggle. She could only cry.

AT FIRST THE DOCTORS THOUGHT MAYA HAD APPENDICITIS AND WERE preparing to do tests when Alice came into the hospital room, coughing.

"I was thinking, then I was reading. Please check her for a spider bite. She may have a black widow spider bite."

They, Stanton included, looked at her skeptically. Stanton headed toward her, hand stretched out, in what looked like an attempt to calm her down.

Alice tried to push him aside and shouted, "Please look! She told me she had a bite."

After a moment, the doctor complied. "Sure enough, lady, looks like she has more than one bite. Are you family?"

"Yes," she said and started to cry.

"We start treating this with muscle relaxers. Robaxin and Valium, then calcium gluconate. The venom attacks the major muscle groups. That's why she's doubled up. If these medicines don't work we'll have to give her the antivenin. I'm thinking she may need it anyway. We'll know soon."

Alice looked at Stanton. "I'm an ambulance chaser," she said. "I watched the ambulance turn in at Maya's."

"Well, good thing you did."

They both looked to the door when Eve Dole walked in with a bouquet of red roses. "How is she?"

"And you are?" asked Alice, protectively.

"Uh...I'm Ms. Valentine's realtor."

"She helped us get in the house," Stanton said. "Maya had the house locked up so tight no one could get in. Thankfully, she had a lock box for the realty company."

Alice turned sharply toward Stanton. "She told me today on the phone that she's not moving. Ever."

"Well gee, we've got a buyer ready to make a good offer, so I hope she is," Eve said, a little harshly to Alice.

Alice started coughing.

Stanton got her some water in a paper cup. "You've got to go home. You've done all you can. Maya needs you to get well."

"I suppose you're right." Alice looked toward Eve, then back at Stanton. "You'll be here for a while won't you, Stanton? She needs to have somebody here."

"Sure. You go rest. I'll call you in the morning."

CHAPTER THIRTEEN

Stanton sat slumped over a magazine, not reading it. His mind focused on why he was here in northeast Oregon in the first place. For his latest book, of course, but this project was different. It came from the love of the stories told to him during his childhood, of being related to a man's man who dared man, weather and beast to find the treasure that awaited him in an unknown land. To learn more about this type of man and to help develop this book that brewed within him, he wanted to be where he'd walked.

Now finally he knew what he could write. It would be fiction based on fact. He'd donate the book's money toward some sort of restoration of the mining area, characterizing it, then making it stay forever. He hadn't figured out how he would characterize it, but he hoped Alice could help him.

It all seemed easy compared to the confusion Maya incited in him. He rubbed the back of his neck and wondered if it was fate that he'd met her. True, he helped her stay alive, but he wondered if it was to be more than that.

Now he wondered how he could think that when she'd taken advantage of him, traipsing around the woods with him in tow, pretending to be a tour guide. When they'd kissed she'd denied him physically. She'd even spit in anger at him.

He thought he'd always wanted a predictable girl and a nice easy life. Maya was far from predictable. No, every time he'd turned around she'd done or said something unexpected. All this rather irked him because he'd thought he knew what he wanted out of life. He realized now he knew nothing.

Except that he cared about this woman, a woman he hadn't even slept with. He shook his head thinking that he would have never thought that was actually possible.

Okay, so he cared about her. What next? She'd get out of here and what? Sell her place? Alice said she wasn't, but that sign in her yard said she was.

He thought about her moving and it brought him down, for he liked the idea of living in northeastern Oregon. He'd searched and finally found a place to call home. This area touched his soul.

His panic attacks were occurring farther and farther apart, and his creative juices flowed well here.

Could he do a long-distance relationship? He'd tried once and it didn't work out. It would be as simple as this: If Maya sold her house he wouldn't pursue her any further.

"Excuse me, are you waiting to see Miss Valentine?" a nurse asked.

He stood. "Yes. Can I see her?"

Maya looked better than the last time he'd seen her. Now, at least, she wasn't doubled up in pain. He touched her hand and her eyes opened.

"You look pale for a gypsy woman."

She smiled, then her eyes clouded up. "I thought I'd seen my dad back at the house, but now I see it was you. You have those same dark eyes."

"Yeah, it was me." He gently pushed the hair back from her forehead and smiled.

"How's Alice?"

"She was here, you know."

"Yeah, I think somebody told me she was. She needed to be home instead."

"True, but wild horses couldn't stop her."

Tears streamed down her face. It touched her that Alice risked all to be here. She felt her love. It felt good.

"Are you okay? Do you hurt?"

She smiled through her tears, thinking men never could understand women's tears. "Actually the absence of pain is pretty nice. I feel like I'm going to be okay. I'm just touched by Alice's concern." Then after he patted the back of her hand she added, "Thanks for your concern, too."

He wanted to see her smile again. "Oh, I'm just here to pick you up. There's a hanging tree I need to go see. I need a tour guide."

"Well, then you're in pretty sad shape, Stanton."

She chuckled through her tears and it softened his heart to her even more. He turned away before he cried as well.

"Hey, Eve Dole stopped by and left you a bouquet. Oh, I see you got it."

"Yeah."

"She said you have a buyer for your house." He turned back to her and watched her eyes, trying to read her face. Her eyes widened, but he could tell it wasn't with excitement.

"Was it Charles Johnson?" she asked.

"She didn't say."

"Did she say where he is? Is he in town?"

"She didn't say," he repeated.

"Would you please hand me my cell? I want to call her."

"Can't this wait until you feel a bit better?"

"No, believe me, it'll help me get better."

"All right." He took the liberty of looking through her contacts for her, then pushed the buttons and handed the phone to her. He tried to brace himself, knowing her future in Salisbury Junction would soon be confirmed.

"Yes, Eve, this is Maya Valentine. Yes, I'm feeling better, thank you. Spider bite, yes. Yes. I understand you have a buyer for my place.

He does. Tell me is he in town? He is. Will you please tell him that I'd like a few days to rest, you understand? Then I'll do business with him... Make sure you tell him exactly what I've said to you... Thank you."

Stanton let out a breath he didn't know he'd held. Well, now Stanton heard it with his own ears. She planned to move. Logically, he should feel better, but he didn't. He reached over and pushed tendrils of hair out of her eyes, then continued to rub his hand over her forehead and hair. His eyes filled up with unshed tears.

Maya thought Stanton looked tortured, but then who wouldn't feel sorry for someone who'd been bitten by black widow spiders, not only once, but twice? When he turned her forearm over and looked at a bite, she knew it was true.

"Thank you," she said near tears again, but she must speak. "I've learned that the worst thing in the world would be to die alone. I can never repay you for making sure that didn't happen."

Then she did cry.

If he hadn't known when she called him "Daddy" hours ago, he knew now how hard she suffered from having lost her parents. Yet, Alice loved her dearly. He suddenly felt guilty for having distrusted Alice, for having thought that Maya deceived him again.

"If you have anyone to thank, it should be Alice. She had a feeling something was wrong and was the one who summoned me." Then at length, he said, "She loves you very much."

"I know." She sniffed. "I'm going to ask Dr. Diethrick to prescribe something different for her cough. Have to keep Alice going. But hey, thanks anyway."

He stepped away from her. "Do you have enough mushroom money to pay for this little adventure?" he asked, changing the subject.

"Yeah. My job's got good medical coverage." Then she remembered she didn't have a job anymore.

"You don't look too convinced."

"Well, I just quit my job. I think I'm covered though for at least another month and then there's that law that allows you to continue with your coverage for a time. I forget what it's called."

She looked up to see furrowed eyebrows. "You quit your job? Has anyone ever told you you're unpredictable?"

"No. What do you mean?"

"Never mind. You need some rest."

Stanton would go down to Admitting and write a check. It would be the last thing he'd do for her. She had done a job for him and was never compensated.

He pulled her set of keys from his pocket. "I took these from your purse, at your house. I thought you'd need them."

"Can you drop them off at Alice's? I'm thinking if she feels well enough, she can go check on Wonder Dog."

"Sure." He kissed her forehead for more than a moment, saying goodbye, not thinking he'd see her again. He picked up her hand, closed his eyes and kissed the palm. Then he left.

Maya watched Stanton leave. She could still feel his lips on her forehead and marveled at how tender and gentle he'd been with her. It not only touched her heart but it moved her to the core of her being. She didn't have the strength to fight the feelings, but instead closed her eyes, took a deep breath and savored them.

After a few moments, she dried her tears with the back of her hand and tried to get comfortable enough to sleep. She looked at her arm and thought how lucky she was to be alive.

CHAPTER FOURTEEN

*M*aya called Alice to tell her she was coming home. Alice agreed to stop by Maya's and open the door for her. She felt much better. Actually they were both feeling better and Maya couldn't help but hum a happy tune on her cab ride home.

BOOMER DIDN'T KNOW WHO HE WAS ANGRIER WITH, EVE OR MAYA. EVE, because she was the bearer of bad news saying Alice Roberts could still be a problem. That Maya was getting awfully close to Alice and she feared the two might never want to part.

She heard it with her own ears that Ms. Roberts didn't want Maya to move. Except he was not to worry, Eve said, since Maya still planned to meet with her.

Women were so friggin' emotional. Women sometimes needed a little help from a man. He left Eve's office abruptly.

Boomer pulled his truck and trailer into the back of Maya's property, then drove his ATV as close to Maya's house as he safely could go without being heard. He took the rest by foot.

After propping an arm against the back of the shed, he picked up a long heavy wrench he'd placed there earlier to use as a weapon in case of emergency. Holding it behind his good leg, he walked to the house.

The door stood ajar and he could see an old woman bending over a dog.

"Alice Roberts?" he asked and she nodded and turned toward him.

He didn't know quite what to say. After a moment, he said, "I'm looking for Maya Valentine. Is she at home?"

"No," she answered. "Who are you?"

He stepped in to better examine her. He could tell that the woman was in poor health. He also knew she looked so frail it wouldn't take much to do her in. He could probably push her over with a feather.

The dog looked friendly enough. He didn't think it'd be a problem. Anyway, he had no qualms about killing a dog or killing another human being for that matter. He learned to do that in 'nam. Adrenaline pumped inside him as he recognized the opportunity God had given him.

"I'm Charles Johnson."

She frowned and shook her head.

Using the wrench, he knocked her down before she'd seen anything coming. Blood began to seep from her head wound and when she moaned in pain, he smiled, thinking about how clever he was to take matters into his own hands. He believed, and never more than at this moment, that if you wanted something done right you had to do it yourself.

With his good leg, he kicked her in the ribs then looked down at the woman. She was very old and her days were numbered. He'd make sure she wouldn't stick around to stop Maya from moving.

While standing at the door, he heard the sound of a car in the distance on the gravel road that intersected with Maya's driveway.

"No!" He'd wanted to make sure the woman was dead but had no chance of that now as he spotted a taxi in the distance. When the taxi signaled to turn, he stealthily slipped out and around the back of the house.

Just as Maya expected, Alice had pulled her car up next to the house. She thought it strange that Wonder Dog just lay on the porch without getting up to greet her. She told the taxi driver to wait only a moment while she went to get money to pay him.

In spite of her call to him, Wonder Dog didn't move until she stood beside him. He acted strangely and she wondered if it was because she'd been gone so much lately.

The door was open a crack and when she pushed it in, she saw Alice sprawled on the floor, blood covering her head.

"Oh, No." Maya's heart pounded. This couldn't be happening. Her knees shook. "Alice. Alice!" she cried. She knelt beside her. Although Alice didn't respond to her touch, she could see her nostrils moving.

Maya let out a sizeable breath of air. "You'll be okay, sweetie."

She pushed Alice's hair out of her face and tried to focus on what she should do. Why couldn't she remember anything from the first aid/CPR class she'd taken the summer before? She had to save her, but what could she do?

"Alice, wake up. You're all I have!" Knowing she needed far more help than what she could provide even with first aid knowledge, she grabbed her phone and called 911.

When she had covered Alice with a blanket, she applied a wet washcloth to the head wound.

At first she thought that Alice had fallen, but on closer inspection believed someone had attacked her. "Oh, who could be heartless enough to hit an old woman?" Nothing made sense anymore. "You'll be okay, Alice. I'm here for you. I love you and you'll be okay," she said soothingly even though Alice didn't respond.

The taxi driver walked in and stared at Alice. "Is the lady okay? Did you get robbed, too?"

"It looks like someone attacked her. I just called 911."

Maya, so consumed with Alice, hadn't thought of the possibility of robbery. In a flash she looked through her things and found that nothing was missing or out of order.

"No, I've not been robbed." She grabbed her purse and paid him.

Not until the ambulance came and loaded Alice did Maya break down. She sobbed watching the paramedic strap Alice onto the stretcher.

"I'll come to the hospital as soon as I can," she told Alice. Alice still did not respond and Maya swallowed a big lump in her throat.

A police car pulled up and a deputy accompanied sheriff Sam Crawford.

"So what are you going to do?" she asked Sam after she told him what happened.

"We're going down to the hospital, hope that Mrs. Roberts will come around and be able to tell us what happened."

Frustration gripped her. "Alice is going to live. She is. What is happening here? What kind of world is this? Who could do this to her? Who could do this to me?"

Sam stood. "Take it easy now. Of course, she'll be all right. We'll get to the bottom of this." He sounded confident, but his glance at his partner belied his words.

Sam was right. She took a deep breath. She'd have to calm down if she intended to recover from her illness, and if she wanted to help Alice.

"I got your call about Charles Johnson being in Arizona," she said. "That's not right. He's in town and planning to do real estate business with me tomorrow."

Sam's partner looked skeptical. "Are you sure about this, ma'am?"

"Yes, because my realtor told me he is."

Sam rubbed his chin. "No, I talked to him in Arizona just before I left you that message."

"What? You talked to him? That's impossible. I saw him when he came to look at my house."

"When I called the Arizona telephone number–Alice Roberts gave me his phone number by the way–he said he didn't know what I was talking about. He hadn't been up here in a while, so he didn't trespass on your property. He said that he had no plans to buy another piece of property. Had things the way he liked them now. He was very convincing."

"Do you have any enemies, Miss Valentine?" his partner asked.

"No." She couldn't think about all this right now. She had to get to the hospital. What little strength she had she'd use to go see Alice. She'd just grab a few things, lock up and leave.

MAYA HAD FALLEN ASLEEP IN A CHAIR NEXT TO ALICE'S HOSPITAL BED. She woke with a crick in her neck. Her eyes focused on a nurse taking Alice's pulse.

She learned that Alice suffered a laceration and concussion from a blow to her head. In addition, she'd sustained bruises and a fracture from a blow to the ribs. A square bandage covered the right side of her head.

Dr. Diethrick thought she'd pull through, having gained consciousness once already and saying her name. She needed time and Maya would take care of her–she just didn't know where. They couldn't go back to her house since they could suffer another attack. Alice's house wouldn't be any safer. She had an apartment in Portland, but neither of them was strong enough to make the trip.

At least Maya felt safe here at the hospital and would just take it a day at a time. Tomorrow she'd have Sam come with her to A and H Realty. They'd get Charles Johnson and maybe that would be the end of things.

Alice finally started to come around and Maya summoned the nurse. She returned with a doctor and he looked in Alice's eyes. "Alice," he said. "Look at me."

Maya didn't know she was holding her breath until the moment Alice focused on him.

"Very good." He continued to poke and prod. Finally, he wrote some things on a chart, mumbled something to the nurse and left.

Maya put her hand on Alice's shoulder and Alice opened her eyes. "Maya."

"Yeah Alice, I'm here." She wanted to ask her some questions about what happened, yet, she didn't want to stress her out. Even the police were holding back until she felt a little more stable. She only patted her hand.

Suddenly Alice's eyes flew open. "Where's Stanton?"

"Well, I don't know, Alice."

"He's not done. He needs more history," she said and then winced. "I feel like I've been run over." She started to cough.

The nurse put a hand on her shoulder. "You need to be still, Mrs. Roberts. Try to relax."

"But I need Stanton," she said as if the nurse surely understood.

"I'll get Stanton for you. Don't worry," Maya said. Heavens, she didn't even know if Stanton was still in town. Moreover, how could she convince him to come back to the hospital, this time to see someone else? Poor guy. They just didn't let up.

Not that she hadn't thought about him. She had. Besides Alice, he was really all she had thought about in the hospital.

Taking her cell phone out of her purse, she stepped into the hall and prayerfully punched in Stanton's number.

"Yeah?"

She let out a breath of relief. "This is Maya."

"Oh, hi. You feeling better?"

"Yeah, uh… It's Alice. She's in the hospital."

"Oh, no."

She figured he knew he was doomed since he couldn't finish his book without Alice's input. She could understand that.

"How she doing?"

"Pretty good for getting beat up."

"Now what are you talking about?"

He obviously did not believe her. It didn't matter. She wouldn't have believed it either. "She was to meet me at my house. When I entered, I found her lying on the floor. Someone attacked her."

"Is she going to be all right?"

"Her doctor seems to think so. With time." She closed her eyes remembering Alice's injuries and then began again, "She wants to see you, Stanton. That's why I called."

"I'm coming. Hang in there."

WHEN STANTON ARRIVED, HE FOUND MAYA STANDING IN THE HALL. SHE didn't look good, not at all. Besides her disheveled appearance, she had dark circles under her eyes.

"Oh good, Stanton. Before you go in, I have to talk to you. You have to be careful what you say to her. Okay?"

"Why? What's going on?"

"She's worried she won't be able to help you finish your book."

"Surely she understands that's she's not well enough to help."

"She's always thought she was well enough to help."

"I find that a little hard to believe. Is she even coherent enough to realize this?"

She sighed. "Some of her first words when she came to were having to do with helping you. She eats and drinks history and her life's ambition is to help you with this book. I am sorry I haven't told you before, but that's why I've been willing to be your tour guide. To help her meet her goals."

"I see." Things were becoming clearer by the moment.

"If you could just placate her, tell her you won't finish your book until she's better. Then when she's well, I'll make amends. Please, she needs a reason to live."

He nodded. He'd been doing his own thinking on his way here. He'd had plans of his own.

Stanton put a hand on Alice's shoulder.

She opened her eyes and smiled at him. "Just looking at you could make a girl heal right up."

"I do what I can." He'd glanced over at Maya and watched her eyes tear up, then turned back to Alice. "I have something to tell you."

Alice's smile vanished. He could tell she was worried.

"Now, you'll like what I have to say. At least I think so and since you're flat on your back, you don't have a choice but to listen.

"I'm going to set up a foundation. It is to be called the *Alice Roberts Foundation* and the funds will come from the book we're putting together. One of the things we need to do is have some interpretive information put on native tuff stone at selected sites. Very hard for anyone to damage or move big rocks, you know. The writing is carved so deep that it'll last many years."

He pulled a chair toward the bed and continued, "It may be possible to make a partnership with the Forest Service and see about moving some remains of some of the historical mines to a park. It's been done before, so we can do it again."

He noticed Maya's jaw was nearly hitting the floor.

MAYA STARED AT STANTON THINKING HE WAS GOING A LITTLE TOO FAR with his story telling. She wished he'd made it a bit simpler. Like he'd wait until she was well enough to finish his book. How she was ever going to explain this away she didn't know. Nevertheless, Alice would have something to live for now.

She looked back at Alice whose eyes were open wide. Now she feared Alice might have a heart attack. She elbowed Stanton aside and leaned over Alice. "Alice this is all well and good, but you need to relax. Put off thinking about this until you've rested."

"This is a good time for me to leave. You rest Alice," said Stanton and slipped out the door.

"Oh, this is wonderful," Alice said as she watched Stanton leave. "Better than I have ever dreamed. Yes, I will rest Maya. Do not worry, I'm okay. But before I rest, I need to talk to the police. I need to tell them–" She coughed and Maya did her best to keep her comfortable.

"You're sure you're ready?" Maya asked, skeptically.

"Got to tell 'em," Alice answered and closed her eyes.

SAM CRAWFORD AND HIS PARTNER, DON PETERS, ARRIVED ABOUT THIRTY minutes later. By that time, Alice was sleeping soundly and they wondered if it was wise to rouse her.

Sam decided they'd waited too long as it was, and Maya knew he was right. Someone had to be held accountable for what Alice had suffered.

"Oh, the sheriff. Yes," Alice said groggily when Sam squeezed her shoulder. In moments, she came fully awake.

"Mrs. Roberts, can you tell me who attacked you?"

"Well, it was a man. I don't know who it was," she answered.

"Okay." Sam took a small pad and pencil from his shirt pocket. "To start, can you tell me what his hair color was?"

"Kind of a salt and pepper color. It was about shoulder length."

"Can you tell me anything else? Anything could help."

"I don't know his eye color." She was silent for a moment, then added, "I think he had a limp."

Sam looked over at Maya.

"Did he look kind of like Willie Nelsen?" Maya asked.

"Yeah, maybe a little."

"Are you sure you've never seen him before?" Sam asked.

"I'm sure."

Sam's partner, Don, stepped forward. "Do you think, Mrs. Roberts, that this man came to see Miss Valentine?"

She thought for a moment and then said. "Yes, I think he was wanting to see Maya. Let me think for a second."

"Take all the time you need," Sam said.

"He asked for Maya. Then he introduced himself."

"You got his name?" Maya asked incredulously.

"No."

"You said he introduced himself, Mrs. Roberts," Sam shot in, frustration evident in his tone.

Alice coughed and her eyes watered. Maya offered the cup of water from Alice's bedside table and Alice lifted her head slightly to take a sip.

"He did. He introduced himself as Charles Johnson," Alice responded clearly.

"So it was Charles Johnson," Maya said to no one in particular.

Alice shook her head. "No, it was not Charles Johnson. I've been a neighbor of Charles Johnson's for years, but when I shook my head in denial, he attacked me. He had enough anger brewing in him that I think he meant to kill me."

Maya was relieved that Sam's partner, Don, planned to stick around the hospital in case "Charles Johnson" found out Alice didn't die and decided to finish the job.

Maya followed Sam out to the hospital corridor. "I think a couple of people in town know this man. One man is named Ryan Allan and the other is named Ed something."

"What makes you think he didn't introduce himself as Charles Johnson to them, too?"

"I don't know that, Sam."

Again, she felt helpless talking to Sam. When he left, she went back to post herself next to Alice. With "Johnson" on the loose, this was her new home, she thought with resignation.

CHAPTER FIFTEEN

Stanton returned with other plans for Maya. He grabbed her bag and motioned for her to join him in the hall.

Maya looked at Alice. She had gone to sleep, quite possibly for the night.

Maya, so tired her eyelids wavered, tried to focus on how she could get rid of Stanton. She'd used him so much and the weight of the guilt made her even wearier. She didn't have enough strength to deal with anything besides how she'd position herself in the chair for the night.

Stanton wouldn't release her bag. She'd even pulled on it. She looked up at him and his lips formed a thin line.

"No money in it," she said.

He smiled. "I'm still not giving it back."

"What do you want?" she asked. "It's getting late."

"I want you to come with me. It's okay. Alice has a guard. She'll be fine. Nothing you can do until morning."

"I can't go with you to Charles Johnson's house. Not after all that's happened."

"What do you mean?"

She put a hand to her forehead and sighed. "Never mind. I'm staying here with Alice."

"No. We're going to go get a room somewhere nearby. Don't look at me like that. I'm nearly as tired as you are."

"But–"

"No buts about it. Your getting some rest will help Alice more than anything else you could do right now."

He was right. She just owed him so much already. She would never get out of debt. Ever.

When she didn't respond, he took her by the hand and led her out of the hospital. Stanton helped her into the passenger's side of his truck and adjusted her seat.

She was so relieved that someone now tended to her that she let herself succumb to her languor. Immediately, she fell into a deep sleep.

Stanton checked into a motel room and ended up carrying her to it.

She was aware enough to notice two queen-sized beds and a kitchenette. He plopped her down on a bed and started to help her undress.

"No." She swatted at his hands. She could do it herself. When she couldn't summon the energy, she said, "One of the good things about being single is you can sleep with your clothes on."

He chuckled and then tucked her, clothes and all, under the covers. She was too tired to sleep.

He'd brought a bag, she noted, when he took it into the bathroom. Then she heard the shower running.

STANTON WAS BEING RECKLESS AND HE MARVELED AT THE CHANGE IN himself. He risked a chance of being caught in a compromising position by the paparazzi. Maybe he was overconfident due to the fact his panic attacks were starting to subside, or because he'd had a reprieve from the gossip mongers here in Salisbury Junction.

When he packed a bag before coming back to the hospital, he'd told himself that among other things, he valued Alice as a historian. A way to help her was to help Maya and he knew Maya in her weakened condition was never so in need of help in her whole life. Knowing Maya wouldn't want to be far from Alice, he decided to find a motel near the hospital for her to stay and recoup for the night.

Stanton thought she'd be asleep by the time he'd finished his shower, but she lay watching him with deeply shadowed eyes. Oh, he hated to see her like this. He missed her strength, her sassiness. He wanted his spitting gypsy back.

"Do you want something to eat?" Stanton asked.

Food. She tried to remember if she had eaten that day or not. She didn't think she had. "I think I could handle some soup."

A short while later, he returned with chicken vegetable soup, a hamburger and fries for himself. The sight and smell of the food made her hungry, and by the time she ate the soup and some of Stanton's French fries, she felt better.

When she couldn't sleep, Stanton gave her an over-the-counter sleeping pill. He lay next to her rubbing her forehead, temple and the top of her head until her eyelids became heavy. Then he crawled into his own bed and turned off the light.

Stanton lay wondering why Maya and Alice had been under attack. Could it be just a neighborhood crime spree? The only connection he could see between the two women was that they were neighbors.

He was the only other connection. He'd been thinking about this and it didn't make sense. After all, nothing had happened to him, besides the grief of seeing two women in pain.

If someone were watching him, wanted to cause him pain, they didn't need to come to Salisbury Junction. If someone hated him that much, they'd be more likely to pursue his family or Michelle Karr.

It all made no sense to him and he was tired. He rubbed his face, then turned over and tried to get some sleep.

When Maya awakened it was nearly noon. After a quick shower, she towel-dried her hair. That was when she noticed the sign on the back of the door. Check-out time was 11:00 A.M. Because of her slackness, they were doomed to pay for another day.

That wasn't her only worry. She had neglected to get over and see Alice this morning.

She started to move quickly, grabbing her bag and dabbing on enough makeup to look alive. A soft tap sounded on the door. Not only had she slept in, she'd monopolized the only bathroom. She grimaced and wrapped an oversized towel around her.

"I'm sorry," she said when she opened the door to Stanton.

At this moment, when he took in the scene with his eyes and his nostrils, he would have given his next book to have her drop the towel to the floor. A little sense of rationality hit him when he looked into her eyes. He was experienced enough to know that they were not expressing the same emotions. The only thing she seemed focused on was getting out of the motel room in a hurry.

"What are you sorry for?" he asked gently. He noted she looked more rested.

She turned from him, slathered some make-up under her eyes and chuckled. "Where do I begin? Sleeping too long, for one."

He stood there, speechless.

"I should have been over to see Alice hours ago. My recent hospital experience helped me learn that it's terribly lonely lying in a hospital bed alone. Some friend I've turned out to be."

"No. You've done the right thing for both of you. You needed rest. You're worthless to her without it. One of you has to be well."

"Look at the time. She's probably worried about me."

"I've been over there twice this morning. She's doing fine."

Stanton watched her finger comb her hair into place. She had wonderful hair. He started to grow crazy from wanting her, but he would not take advantage of a sick woman. A sick woman who's had

a lot of emotional upheaval in her life lately. For this reason, he felt
it important to step back as politely as he could. He didn't gather
her in his arms when she attempted to give him a hug for visiting
Alice.

Her eyes darted to his face in question, then her face turned red
and her lips thinned.

He was in big trouble and he didn't know why. He frantically
searched his mind for their last interchange. It was fine. She had
thanked him and tried to give him a hug, but he'd respectfully pulled
away.

Suddenly he realized he'd spurned her when he didn't return her
hug and it must have hurt her ego. Yet he was only trying to be nice.
"I'm not rejecting you," he said softly.

He stood there until she grew serious. They made eye contact and
he held her gaze, then smiled.

Suddenly, she realized the impropriety of wearing only a towel.
She put a hand on her chest and his eyes followed her hand. It wasn't
hard to see if she tried to hug him now, he wouldn't pull away.

She wanted to have him care beyond charity and beyond sex. She
so didn't want to be a bittersweet memory, yet they weren't anywhere
near a commitment of any kind.

"I don't know what to do," she said more to herself than to him. "I
don't want to be just a conquest, Stanton," she added, finding it hard
to look back at him.

He sighed. "Look at me, Maya." When she did, he could easily read
in her eyes that she wanted to connect with him in all ways, not just
physically. Would he ever understand her? How could she want this
when she'd planned to move away? Didn't she say she had an appointment with her realtor today? He didn't want a long-distance relationship.

Finally, he said, "I guess I don't know what to do either, Maya."

It was easy with Alice. He'd just promised her an institute. He had
nothing to give Maya, nothing to give this special woman. He
smoothed back the hair from her face. His gaze moved over the swell
of her breasts, visible above the towel. He backed away and stood by

the motel door for a few minutes listening to the sounds of Maya dressing in the bathroom.

BOOMER HAD BEEN SURPRISED, THEN DISPLEASED THAT HE HADN'T killed Mrs. Roberts. He'd just not planned on having to give her another thought. Well, she didn't know who he was, so he wasn't in any danger.

She could wait. He needed to find out what Maya was doing. Thinking she was probably by Alice's side, like a good little girl, he had searched for her there.

After arriving at the hospital, he'd found that very few were allowed to visit Mrs. Roberts. If the nurses did not stop him, the police officer he spotted at her door would.

His latest plan came through divinely when from the parking lot that evening, he'd watched Stanton take Maya away from the hospital to a motel. He used his phone to call two magazines.

That bastard did not deserve the respect he received. The public needed to know he was a no good, son-of-a-gun with the morals of an alley cat.

As he watched the press arrive at the motel, he thanked God and quoted a Bible verse. "Take heed that ye stand, lest ye fall."

WHEN STANTON OPENED THE DOOR OF THE MOTEL ROOM HE FROZE. There stood the press, reminding him of vultures hovering over their prey. It was a sight he'd seen before, but would never get used to.

He remembered another time he'd encountered them. Michelle was on his arm. They'd just left a restaurant in New York and were headed to his agent's office when a man with a camera stepped in front of them blocking their path.

The camera flashed right in his face and he was without sight for a few moments. While blinded he felt hands on his body, Michelle being pulled from his arm while people tried to talk to them, many voices at once. When he tried to protect himself by pushing people away from their personal space, they took it as rejection and verbally belittled them as they scurried away from the crowd.

The fears that assailed him were many. What if someone wanted a hunk of Michelle's hair, or wanted to fondle her, hurt her or steal her away? He knew firsthand there were nuts out there and something could happen. He felt totally helpless in a crowd of many, blinded by cameras and pushed at so hard he couldn't protect himself let alone Michelle.

Without a word, he shut the door, then checked the lock. Even if there were no nuts out there, even one good picture could give a photographer a nice paycheck. Enough money to make a man willing to get their prey riled up, doing something foolish to make the tabloids.

Stanton sighed, wondering if he should tell Maya why he wanted such a private life, about the panic attacks and about what has happened to him due to his fame. But it would frighten her, and she needed to have courage to face the other side of this door.

"Maya, it's the press." He met her at the bathroom door. "Do you know anything about this?"

His tone wasn't accusing, simply inquiring. Maya shook her head. Besides Alice, who could possibly have known where they were? Alice was next to dead, secluded and under police protection. Obviously she wouldn't be the culprit. Perhaps Stanton inadvertently told someone.

"Should we wait this out?" she asked.

"No. They could stake this place out for days. We'll just go on with our lives."

When he looked at her, she thought she saw regret in his eyes and felt it, too.

"I'll drop you off at the hospital and then I'll go get us some lunch," he said.

"I'm not very hungry."

"You'll eat. You've got to keep your strength."

"Yes. You're right," she answered.

He rubbed his face as if in frustration, then turned to her. "Get dressed. Let's get out of here."

"I'll just be a minute."

Stanton grabbed her arm and then braced himself for what was on the other side of the door. Just watching him take a breath, then strengthen his hold, caused an adrenaline-laced fear to run through her body.

When the lights flashed in her eyes, her heart pounded. She looked down as Stanton pulled her along behind him at a fast pace. Voices reached her, many jumbled together. Someone mentioned Michelle Karr.

Stanton's fiancé. Stanton hadn't wanted to talk about Michelle and Maya herself had gotten good at pushing Michelle into the recesses of her mind, but she couldn't stay in denial forever.

"No comment," she heard Stanton say several times and then he took her arm again. Next, he put her into his pick-up, policeman style with his hand over her head. Cameras continued to flash, causing spots to dance whether her eyes were open or closed.

"Now do you see why I've been so quiet about my life?" Stanton said as he pulled away from the motel.

She did see. "Yes."

He looked at her and then shook his head. "I've had stories in my head. I only wanted to write them and share them with others. That's all. I had no idea I could become famous, or of what the business side of it all could amount to."

She could hardly feel sorry for him for getting what so many people have only dreamed. "To be able to gain from your talent is a good thing, Stanton."

He only scowled at her.

Looking out the window, she thought of her rulebook. She knew if she'd followed the guidelines she had for her life, she'd be above reproach. It seemed obvious to her that Stanton had no guidelines.

"Since you're in the limelight, it would seem to me that you'd want to watch your *P's* and *Q's*," she said, then closed her eyes waiting for the hatchet to fall.

"No one's going to tell me what to do and how to act, Maya. What kind of life is that?" he returned, his voice a little higher.

She feared she was stomping on holy ground, but she cared about the man and had to know. "Even if by doing what you want hurts someone else. Like Michelle, for instance?"

After pulling into the hospital parking lot and finding a space to park, he turned off the pickup. "What Michelle means to me is only business."

Business or no, Maya could tell he didn't like her delving into his life. She noted sadly that it hurt her feelings, but she wasn't going to cry. No, she was going to get mad instead.

"Business, huh?" she said, her voice rising.

"Yes, business," he stated, seemingly satisfied that she now understood.

She thumbed her chest. "Just like I'm business, huh, Stanton? After all, I'm your tour guide. Thank goodness for the press interrupting our business transaction. The last transaction, I might add."

"Wait," Stanton said, trying to get a grip on her clothing to keep her from getting out of the truck. She squirmed lose and stepped outside.

"Goodbye, Stanton. Thanks for everything."

"Wait," he said again, louder this time.

"Don't worry, I won't leak anything to the press. Mum's the word."

She didn't turn to watch him leave but headed straight ahead, tears streaming down her face. She was just glad he didn't see her cry.

By the time Maya reached Alice's hospital room she'd managed to control her emotions. It pleased her to see Alice's condition had improved and that Sam Crawford leaned over her, displaying what looked like pictures of known criminals.

Alice looked up as she came into the room with the sweetest grin. Maya decided she would freeze frame that smile in her memory.

"Where's Stanton?" Alice asked, seemingly surprised he wasn't behind her.

As Maya figured, Stanton must have told her she was with him last night. Too bad she was going to have to burst Alice's bubble about their being a couple. "He's a busy guy. Got to get back to the writing, you know."

Alice seemed satisfied. "Come look at these pictures." She waved her closer. The two of them looked at what appeared to be criminal mug shots, which were displayed in any post office across the country. None looked familiar.

Sam left the room since Alice expected her doctor. Maya told her she would be leaving too, but didn't say she was going to the real estate office. She didn't think it mattered. Alice's eyelids started to droop. She was probably ready for a nice, long nap.

What better way to keep her thoughts off Stanton, she decided, than by keeping the appointment with Eve and her prospective buyer? Maya was glad her car hadn't been impounded. She'd left it in the hospital parking lot overnight.

She had so much on her mind she'd forgotten to tell Sam about the appointment. No problem, she'd just call him from Eve's.

When Maya turned the doorknob at Eve Dole's office, her heart pounded. The Willie Nelsen look-a-like sat next to Ms. Dole's desk. He had a few days growth of whiskers and salt and pepper hair, unkempt around his shoulders. An empty chair sat opposite him.

She stopped to take a breath and then continued over to them, telling herself repeatedly to remain calm. She patted her back pocket. Her cell was not there.

"Oh, there you are, Ms. Valentine. Right on time," Eve said and stood, extending her hand. "I was beginning to think this deal wouldn't come to fruition."

Maya had only seen her at a distance before, having put her house for sale via email, so she studied the woman's features. She was as she'd pictured her, a slender woman with harsh makeup and bleached blonde hair. She appeared to be in her early fifties.

"Well, as you know I've had a few setbacks lately," Maya answered with a smile and a handshake.

"This is Charles Johnson. I don't think you've met."

He stood, smiled and took her extended hand.

When their hands touched, a shiver ran down her spine. She hoped he didn't notice her repulsion.

"No, I've not met Mr. Johnson." She tried to turn from the man as nonchalantly as she could. "May I use your phone?"

Charles squirmed in his chair. "If we could just do this business first," he insisted.

Eve looked at Charles. "Well, perhaps he's right. If we could get this finished as Mr. Johnson has another appointment in a little bit."

Yeah, Maya thought, like beating up more defenseless old women. She didn't think Johnson would try and harm her while Eve was in the room. Still, how was she going to get any kind of help? Somehow, she'd have to make Eve see that he wasn't who he claimed to be. Perhaps then she'd have an ally.

"How's Arizona, Mr. Johnson?" Maya asked.

Eve's eyebrows furrowed in question as she shot a look at the man.

"I like Oregon better. For one, Eve lives here."

Eve smiled at that, patted his hand and then kept it there.

This was highly unethical, Maya thought. Why would Eve flaunt a relationship with a buyer if she was representing the seller? Eve wasn't even thinking straight. She'd heard of women choosing the wrong kind of man, but geez, this took the cake.

"I see," she said. Her hopes of an affiliation with Eve were nil. How she wished she'd been nicer to her in the past.

Maya sat quietly for a few moments, eyeing the phone as if it was a piece of chocolate. Eve must have noticed in that her eyebrows furrowed again and with it came the look of annoyance.

"Eve, would you bring the papers forward?" Charles asked.

"Certainly."

Maya glanced over the papers laid before her, checking the name, C. A. Johnson. "So, Mr. Johnson, you want to add this to your property that borders mine?"

"I have plans for this property, if that's what you're asking."

"Like?" *Blasting a hole to China*, she thought.

"Personal plans."

"Now, Ms. Valentine," Eve said, "we're not going to go through this thing about the best possible owner again, are we? Now I realize you have a sentimental attachment to the property, but it's only a piece of land for goodness sake."

Maya wanted to smack her. It wasn't just a piece of land. It was her father's haven, her family's haven. If Eve thought she'd just hand it over to this savage, she had another thing coming.

Perhaps she could approach Eve as a businessperson. After all, Eve was her real estate agent. If she could get her alone, then she could rationally explain her objections to Charles and get a chance to call the police.

Maya tried to smile, "Oh, of course not. I was just making conversation. I do notice that this figure is a little lower than I'd hoped. Can I talk to you privately, Eve?"

Having talked to Eve many times on the phone, Maya would have bet her property she would never be anything but professional. Although the way she looked at Charles now, as if he were an angel, then back to Maya, as if she were the devil, certainly made her wonder.

Eve sighed. "Okay. Charles, could you please step into the other room for a second? Just for a second."

Maya watched Charles limp into what looked like another office. She sighed inwardly. Now, maybe she could get somewhere. Her palms were sweating and she rubbed them on her jeans.

"How well do you know this man?" she whispered.

"Very well," said Eve.

"You believe he is who he says he is?"

Now she sparked some emotion. "Why of course. Now if you're concerned about the financing going through, then I would have you return to the form in front of you. My name is under his, do you see?"

Maya was appalled. "You're going to go into a partnership with this man?"

"I'm hoping, in every way possible." Eve's voice was stiff.

Maya looked to the closed door behind which Charles waited and her heart started to pound again. She was sure he had no qualms about hurting her if she didn't succumb to his wishes.

She wondered what happened to the angry, spitting gypsy she became around Stanton. In the scheme of things, she realized how trivial sparing with Stanton was. If she got out of this in one piece, she was determined to apologize to him for becoming angry those many times. Now, when she really should be fighting mad, she was not. If she could find a corner to whimper in, she'd take it.

She leaned back and took a deep breath, wondering who could help her now? She couldn't be helped because she'd told no one about how crucial this meeting was. She'd been closed-minded about telling Stanton anything. Not that he should help her, again, but he probably would've convinced her to consult the police.

Without a soul to help, she thought her only way out of all this mess was to sell lock, stock and barrel, to these two creeps. Her father would probably turn over in his grave to have his property taken this way, not to mention seeing his daughter hurt or taken advantage of.

However, Johnson wasn't hurting her yet. She could still use her mental resources to end this mess but she found herself drawing a blank. She grasped at straws when she said, "About that call I wanted to make. I think maybe Stanton Black can give me more money than you're offering. Now, you're my real estate agent, so you could bene-fit, too. Uh–that is if you help me get more money for my property."

Eve shook her head. "We've already got funds allocated for this, this down payment."

"Nothing is legally binding yet. Isn't that right, Eve?"

Eve was quiet for more than a moment. Putting a hand on her heart, she leaned forward and said, "Please understand, this tract of land means everything to Charles. It's his dream property. It's what's keeping him here. Here with me."

That sounded like a personal problem to Maya, but she thought it was wise not to say so. "I do understand, but I have my own needs, too. Let's just say we get Stanton over here and if he doesn't see fit to cough up any more money, then it's yours." She pointed to the next room. "Ah... And his."

Eve rubbed her temples, then looked up at Maya. "First, I believe this is a fair price. Second, I don't believe Mr. Black is after this piece. We could probably just call him and ask. I doubt he needs to come out here tonight."

Maya's first hope of the day sprang forward. "Okay."

New worries evolved around what she would say to Stanton. She needed to be especially careful of her wording with Eve nearby. Moreover, what good would it do for him to come out here? She needed the police. She needed Sam Crawford. Too bad Sam wasn't looking for real estate.

He answered the phone. "Stanton? This is Maya. You know we talked about your wanting property in this area? Yes, well I'm here with Eve Dole at her office. Eve and I have been talking about your interest in buying something in the area. I think my property fits your needs and I'd like you to join us now. No, I'm not making this up. No. It would be okay to bring your dog, Sam, along if you'd like."

Eve had been tapping her foot and then she rudely took the telephone from her hand and Maya jumped and shrieked, startled by the interaction.

Putting the phone to her breast, Eve said to Maya, "I'm sorry, but this is irrational and highly unprofessional. Mr. Black is an important client of mine. He doesn't need to make a trip out here. If you want to see him, do it on your own time, okay?"

If it wasn't for ol' Charles Johnson in the other room, Maya would have slapped her royal. So she was irrational? Who wouldn't be, meeting up with the likes of Eve and her darling Charles? She'd believed the woman was professional. Pooh. She was a man=crazy old biddy thinking only of herself.

Maya rubbed her face with her hands in a calming effort, then looked up and listened to what Eve was saying to Stanton.

"Sorry to bother you, Mr. Black. I know you're a busy man. Miss Valentine here seems to think you might be interested in her property. Have you seen it?"

Maya knew she told Eve that he had. Obviously, she believed her to be nothing but an obsessed fan.

"Oh you have," said Eve and Maya inwardly smirked. "Yes," Eve continued, "we seem to have another offer on this property and he's just twitching to sign the papers."

Maya leaned forward, suddenly believing she had a good idea. "Tell him who it is."

Eve blatantly ignored her, turning in her swivel chair toward the window. "So you're not interested then." Eve turned back toward Maya with a smile. "Yes, sorry to bother you then."

"What was that outburst all about?" Eve asked when she'd set the phone down.

"Just thought he might be interested in knowing his landlord wanted the property is all."

Maya's plan failed. It hurt her that Stanton wouldn't do what she'd asked and the tears came unbidden. "Now, what am I going to do?" she mumbled to herself.

Eve leaned forward and said, "What does that mean, Maya? What's really going on here?" She said the words smoothly and then stood. When Maya didn't answer she said, "I suppose I'd better get Charles."

The way Eve had spoken frightened Maya. "Wait, it's just that I have a crush on Stanton. I mean, who wouldn't? He's gorgeous. Wait just a second before you get Mr. Johnson. I need to dry my eyes, compose myself and ask questions about the paperwork here."

CHAPTER SIXTEEN

*S*tanton hung up the phone and wondered what Maya was up to now. She certainly didn't lead a boring life. He'd give her that. It was hard to believe she wanted him to just drop everything and get to the real estate office. What kind of business was that?

Furthermore, it should have been Eve making the call, perhaps with a message to update him on what was on the market. Did Maya actually think this was some kind of auction?

He walked over to a window and stared out toward the Valentine property. Not being able to see the house from this angle, he turned and went over the two conversations he'd just had.

Even though he liked the Valentine property, he was not going to give Maya the justice of being her means of leaving town. No, there had to be some other piece of land out there with his name on it, without emotional ties.

Just about to dismiss the whole thing from his mind, he thought about the last thing Maya said. He was sure she'd said he could bring his dog. The woman had to be crazy. She knew he didn't have a dog. A dog she'd even had a name for, for Pete's sake. He shook his head and then unsuccessfully tried to recall the name she'd given the dog.

AFTER SAM CRAWFORD HAD A BITE TO EAT, HE HEADED BACK TO THE hospital. The Alice Roberts case troubled him and he had more questions to ask.

He'd hoped to see Maya, for he'd been feeling guilty lately for not helping her enough with this case. But what could he do? So far he'd done what he'd been trained to do. It just wasn't enough, that's all.

Then he remembered Maya told him she knew of two others who could help identify this man. Perhaps she had something. That is, if the two would cooperate. Sometimes people were funny, especially in a small town. If you got involved in trouble, the whole town would read about it in the daily paper. Some people just didn't want to become that well-known.

At the hospital, he found Alice asleep. He sat down beside the bed waiting for her to wake and for Maya to return. When Maya hadn't answered her phone, he wondered where she could be.

Sam was half way through a Reader's Digest when Alice began to stir. She looked up at him and blinked. He smiled and set the magazine down.

"How are you feeling, Mrs. Roberts?"

"Like I've been beat up." After a moment, she added, "I think my cough's better though. Where's Maya? Have you seen her?"

"No. I thought she might turn up here. Did she say where she might be going today? With this guy on the loose, I'm a little worried about her being out and about."

He wished he hadn't added that last comment when Alice frowned. She started to rise and it made him nervous. He pushed the button for the nurse and then tried to get her to lie back down.

Alice did lie down and muttered something about Stanton.

"What did you say, Mrs. Roberts?"

"I said that she's probably not with Stanton. She said he was home trying to write, I think."

Sam ran a hand through his hair. Not a lot of things to do in Salisbury Junction, especially to keep Maya away for such a long period of time.

"You know it's odd she's not here, Mr. Crawford. I'm starting to get concerned."

The look Alice gave Sam reminded him of a little girl looking to her daddy for help. He didn't want to disappoint her, but he'd been in the business long enough to know he couldn't fix everything because he had a badge.

"Did she have any kind of business to attend to? Can you think of anything?" he asked.

Alice shook her head, then after a moment told him that Maya's house was up for sale and that Maya said she'd decided not to sell after all. That was the only business she could think of.

"Do you know who her realtor is?" Sam asked hopefully.

"That Eve Dole woman," Alice answered bitterly.

Sam knew her. Didn't think too highly of her either. "I don't want you to be concerned, Mrs. Roberts. I'll just wait here until Maya returns. Then we'll all hash this case out and be done with it. How does that sound?"

Alice nodded and Sam smiled.

Boomer had been listening at the door in the office of A and H Realty. He couldn't believe that Maya was the average client. She was too nervous and asked too many questions. He'd given her plenty of time so he could figure out what was up her sleeve.

Thankfully, Eve was a woman in love. Yeah, she was all he wanted in a woman, devoted and desperate enough to stand by her man. She was not going to put up with this idiot of a girl trying to get out of this deal. Especially a deal that Eve knew would mesh the two of them together.

Maya wasn't cooperating at all. He'd have to intervene himself. When he yanked on the door handle, the door stuck and then made a cracking noise when it opened with force.

MAYA SCREAMED, THEN TURNED WITH HER HAND ON HER HEART.

"I've been meaning to get that fixed," Eve said with a chuckle. "Now, Ms. Valentine, I can see that you're as anxious as we are to get out of here, so why don't you sign these papers and be off?"

"Sounds good to me," Charles said, now standing behind Maya.

Maya looked from one to the other and then tried to remember if there was some kind of clause where she could get out of this within so many days if she so chose. There had been such a clause when she bought a new car. Surely there would be one for something much more expensive.

"How would that work legally," she asked Eve, "if I decide, say tomorrow, that I didn't want to sell after all?"

Boomer had heard enough. "No, you will sell. That's all there is to it. You will sell."

He'd said it rather gruffly and she caught Eve giving him a questioning look. "Actually, there is a clause," Eve told him.

"No, there's not," he shot back trying to get the upper hand.

Seeing the way the last comments registered on Eve's face, Maya thought maybe she had nothing to lose if she brought out some more of the brute in him. She pretended to ignore him. "Oh, there is then, Eve. Good."

"No there's not," he said and slapped his hand on Eve's desk.

Considering his abuse to Alice, Maya was not surprised to see this anger, but obviously Eve was.

"May I talk to you privately, Charles?" Eve asked.

"The name's C.J. and no you may not. I have things to do today, so we need to get these papers signed. Let's get going here."

"What?" Eve said. "You want me to call you C.J. and you're just now telling me this?"

He didn't respond but stared blankly at her.

Maya took a deep breath and then dared to speak. "But Mr. Johnson, I only want to know the business side of this, that's all. It's what every liberated woman should know, right?"

"Every woman should know nothing. From what I can see here today, women don't know anything. You're not cut out for this, Eve. I am, and I say we sign this and be done with it."

Maya looked at Eve, hoping she wasn't the kind of fool she'd just minutes ago thought she was.

"Mr. Johnson," Eve began in a rigid tone, "I've succeeded as a businesswoman in this town on my own merits. No man has helped me."

"No man would help you."

Eve stood. "I've changed my mind, Ms. Valentine. I want this property all right, but I only want it in my name. Sure, I'll pay a little more for it if you like since it's good riverfront property."

Johnson yanked his shoulders back. "No, you won't."

"Well, it looks like I'm the only option in this room since you can't get the financing without me," Eve said, thumb to chest.

Maya dared to say in all seriousness, "Do you really want it, Eve?"

"Well, yes. I've been planning all along to break up the property, sell it in pieces along the river and make a bundle on it. Then I'd leave this God-forsaken town."

By the emotions exhibited on Eve's face, Maya knew those words were meant to wound Johnson.

"You hadn't told me you'd planned to do that," he said.

"It was always a plan in the back of my mind if things didn't work out between us."

He shook his head. "No. This property will stay in one piece, at least for now. I'm not going to saddle myself to that woman to be able to get it."

"Then just what are you going to do to get it?"

"You're going to sign it. Both of you."

Eve laughed. "You can't make us."

Just then, Johnson stormed out of the office and Maya let out a huge sigh of relief. Eve started crying. Then Johnson barged in, holding a gun.

"Sign it, damn it." He jabbed the gun at them.

Numb with fear and defeat, she bent over to sign the papers. She focused on her name and it steadied her. Maya Valentine. She'd wanted a different name growing up, but now she was proud to have her father's name and his beloved property. She took a deep breath.

This man lived in some sort of fantasy world if he believed she'd sign away the Valentine property. If he could live a fantasy so could she, and she scribbled, *Mrs. Stanton Black*. She knew Johnson was too anxious to get out of the real estate office to stop and check the authenticity.

"You can't get away with this. You're crazy, do you know that?" Eve cried.

Maya couldn't believe it when he smashed his fist into the side of Eve's head. She crashed behind her desk and lay still.

With heart pounding and hands shaking, Maya still managed to flip every page and scribble the fantasy name.

Charles exploded into a tirade about Vietnam. And when he stopped talking, she looked up to see him staring at something out the window. She followed his gaze and saw Stanton pull into the parking lot.

AFTER STANTON RECEIVED THE CALL FROM MAYA, HE WASN'T ABLE TO resume writing. He went down to the river for inspiration, but could think of nothing but Maya.

With a sigh, he walked over to the place where he'd seen her the first time. He was sure he'd thought of nothing else but her since that moment.

He kicked at a stone, sending it skimming across the river. Oh, how she frustrated him. He hated the way she occupied his every waking moment. He couldn't write any more, couldn't sleep. Maybe they should have a talk and both explain what they wanted from each other.

He stared up at her house, noting the for sale sign. Maybe she didn't want anything from him. If she cared a whit for him, then why was she moving away?

While it was easy to leave him, how could she leave Alice, whom she loved? He supposed she'd be back to check on her. Perhaps then he would see her, from time to time. No, he wouldn't attempt to see her. Not if she could just up and leave him as she'd planned.

She thought he should be the one to buy her property. Not only that, she wanted him to come down at that precise moment and sign her off. She just had a lot of gall, that woman. He was surprised she didn't ask him to pack her bags, too, and send her on her way.

She'd even made up that stupid comment about his having a dog. Unpredictable she was, but what kind of fool idea was that to get him to come running?

He had to admit her life had not been easy in Salisbury Junction. He'd give her credit for that. Her house had been broken into, her beloved Alice attacked by a man who supposedly owned the house he lived in. People had moved for less.

Looking out toward Alice's, he spotted Wonder Dog and smiled. It was amazing that through all this the old dog was still surviving.

Stanton wondered if Sam cracked the case yet.

Awareness swept over him. "No. No!" He made a wild dash to his house.

STANTON LEAPT FROM HIS TRUCK. IN AN INSTANT, HE REACHED THE REAL estate office door.

Johnson yanked Maya up from her chair and shoved her under his arm. She kicked at his leg but he only laughed, saying she was stupid to kick an artificial limb.

"Yeah, I got this here new leg fighting for you and my country, sweet dear."

The smell of stale liquor nearly gagged her. When she tried to squirm away, he touched her head with the nozzle of the gun. "Don't you think Mr. Black here is going to try and save you because he's not."

"I don't need saving, Mr. Johnson. Just let me go and we'll finish this deal. You'll get your land. We'll just tell Mr. Black to go away."

"Don't worry Ms. Valentine, no one will come between me and this piece of property. Not your father, you and not Stanton Black."

Maya felt fear deeper than she'd ever experienced before.

Stanton pushed the door open. When Johnson pointed the gun at him, he held up both hands. "Who are you?" he asked. "What is it you want? If it's money, I can give you some. Just leave Maya out of this."

"Oh, but I can't leave Maya out of this. She means everything to me."

Stanton looked at Maya in question and Johnson tightened his grip on her. "Let me do the talking, dear. The name's Johnson. C.J. Johnson."

Maya could see Stanton surveying the room, his eyes widened when he spotted Eve passed out on the floor. "How much money do you need, Mr. Johnson?"

"Your money? Take heed you stand, lest you fall!" Johnson shouted. "You don't deserve the fame you have. You've done nothing for the country that keeps you free. You've only written a few books. You don't deserve the woman you have."

Johnson's voice rose to such a fevered pitch that Maya thought her heart was going to jump out of her throat. It was the shriek of a mad man.

"God will see that you get your just rewards, my man. You will not get this land or the woman you love. You're a fornicator, one more reason you're not entitled to get her."

Maya wondered about many things. She understood about Johnson wanting her land, but how he could possibly think that Stanton loved her was irrational.

"She's mine," Johnson said.

Maya stiffened, horrified.

"Mr. Johnson, I don't know you very well, so how can I be yours?"

Johnson laughed hard and his grip loosened a bit. Thankfully, she could breathe a little better.

"How pitiful you are. Black here doesn't love you. He's only been whiling away the hours with you."

183

The comment didn't really concern her since she thought some of those same thoughts herself, but Stanton looked furious.

"No. You're wrong, I've realized I do love Maya."

Maya wondered what Stanton was up to. Why in the world did he need to lie?

Johnson hugged her so tightly that all air rushed out of her lungs. "That's blasphemy, pure and simple!"

Maya tried to think how she could play on Johnson's sick delusion that he loved her. "I had no idea you cared for me, Charles."

"The name's C.J.," he roared and she blinked. "No, it's not you I care about."

Then it must be Eve, she thought. Yet, Eve would hardly be someone Stanton would be after and Johnson didn't act like he cared about her one bit, either.

She thought she was helping, trying to get Johnson to see the light, when she said, "Stanton you haven't been seeing Eve have you?"

Stanton looked over at Eve lying on the floor. "No. Believe me, C.J., no," he answered gently. "By the way, don't you think we should help her?"

"Ha! Why should I help her. She didn't help me. She's a self-supporting feminist. She doesn't need any man," he said with a sneer.

Okay, so it wasn't Eve. She had no answers, nothing at all to go on. All she had was a multitude of questions. "She can't lie there forever. He's right. She needs help. What are you planning to do, C.J.?"

"I'm going to eliminate everyone who is standing in my way. The way to riches, my recognition and my woman."

———

STANTON LOOKED OVER AT EVE AND SAW HER MOVE EVER SO SLIGHTLY. Thank goodness she was alive.

He'd never felt this helpless in his entire life, but he had to find a way to help Maya.

This man, this Johnson, was not Charles Johnson his landlord. He hadn't met Charles, only dealt with him by phone, mail and email, but he'd seen a good likeness of him in a picture in the bedroom.

This man was nuttier than a fruitcake. Logic would not win out this time. He'd gotten himself in very deep without a weapon, not even a pocketknife to save him. What had he been thinking? He'd assumed his money or notoriety could save him, but these things were obviously offensive to Johnson.

This "Johnson" thought he knew all about him, but Stanton knew he hadn't ever met him. It was not altogether too surprising that he'd have knowledge of him. He was in the media from time to time.

He quickly realized that he was a threat to him and wasn't sure why. He said he didn't love Maya or Eve, so who did that leave? Had they dated the same woman? He thought that highly unlikely. He also doubted he was a father or sibling of someone he knew. The name Johnson, however common, didn't ring any bells.

"Are you a brother to Charles Johnson?" Stanton asked.

"No. Charles is just a means to an end."

He couldn't possibly know what that meant. "Do you have a relative that I might know?"

"No." Johnson said and smirked, then added, "My relatives don't claim me."

Maybe it was someone from the entertainment world, someone he didn't even know. After all, this man was nuts. He thought quick and hard and came up with one name: Michelle Karr.

"PLEASE, YOU CAN HAVE MY LAND. STANTON, HE'S FOUND GOLD ON MY property. That's why he wants it," said Maya.

"Yes, and it was divine intervention that caused me to find it, too. It's meant to be mine. All I had to do was go through the steps. Now God will award me with everything that's due me."

Prison, she hoped. "Steps you say? How can I be involved in these steps? These steps to help a veteran, someone who has fought for his country."

Johnson looked hard at her for a moment. "I see you're starting to understand. Your old man, he didn't understand. That's why I had to get rid of him."

"My father?" Her voice was small and pitiful.

"Yes, he was step two. Step one was finding the gold in the first place."

She didn't know if she could get the questions out since her throat was constricting. "Did you say he didn't understand?"

"No. He wouldn't sell. I had to convince him otherwise. He didn't die of a heart attack. God chose to strike him down. It was divine, you know, since no one found out. I'd just slipped him a concoction a medic friend of mine made. I told the people in his office that he'd clutched at his heart, then went down. It was as simple as that."

Now Maya knew she was going to die, too, over land and gold.

"If I die, how do you know someone won't trace it to you?"

"That's where Charles Johnson comes in, sweetie. Just came in handy when I checked the tax records and found a Johnson on the neighboring property. It's surprising how many gents in town don't even know him. Guess it's 'cause he's gone a lot. First name even starts with a C. How divine is that, may I ask you? Yep, Charles will take the blame for any wrongdoing. At least for a while, until I'm long gone. God will take care of the rest. Now, the way it's all coming together, I'd say it was meant to be. Wouldn't you?"

"Yes, I understand. Too much to be coincidence." She realized the predicament they were all in and what she valued right then was for Stanton and Eve to leave. Not so much for getting help, for she didn't even know that help could be gotten in time to save her, but to keep the two of them alive.

"No C.J., this is between me and you, so why don't you just let Stanton and Eve go. They aren't part of God's plan."

"Oh, but they are. Well, not Eve so much as Black here. He stands in the way of my love and I."

STANTON REALIZED THAT JUST AS MAYA HAD BEEN CAREFUL IN GAINING Johnson's trust, likewise, he would have to be careful how he handled the topic of Michelle Karr.

"She doesn't love me, you know," said Stanton, quietly and gently.

Johnson looked offended and now pointed his gun back at Stanton. "What do you mean? What are you trying to say?"

Stanton took a deep breath. "I'm saying that Michelle loves another. She didn't say who, so now I'm thinking it must be you."

"Don't talk about her that way. Do not talk about her like that. She's a good woman, just blinded by the likes of you. You think you can smooth talk me and get out of here, but I'll tell you something. Michelle hasn't even met me yet."

"I don't understand," Stanton said, truly confused.

"Michelle is the last step. After I've gotten all my gold, then I'll go get Michelle. Along with her comes all the long-awaited recognition for my time in 'nam. I won't miss you this time. No, I'll shoot you right between the eyes. Michelle, she'll be mourning your loss, but about that time she'll be ready for another man. A man who will treat her good and be faithful to her, not shack up in some motel like you just did with Maya."

Stanton tried to look like he calmly focused on what the madman was saying while concluding that Johnson was the one that told the media to come to the motel. He also noticed he held the gun with his left hand, and when he'd jerked Maya around in his madness, he had a limp.

This man had chased him that foggy night that now replayed in his dreams.

Barely audible was the crushing of gravel outside. Stanton would have to think quickly. The time to move was upon him.

MAYA NOW SAW HOW THEY ALL TIED TOGETHER. A LUNATIC HAD doomed every one of them. He'd nearly killed Alice and could try it again since she'd live right next door to him. Right next door where he could hide out in the back of the property and no one would be the wiser.

She felt sure Stanton was to die after herself, for gaining Michelle's attention and earning recognition and fame. Maya could almost see the wheels turning in Stanton's head, his trying to create the perfect rescue scene, and then frustration when he could not.

He said that he loved her, but she believed it was only to placate Johnson. When she looked at him now, she realized she loved Stanton very much and couldn't help the tears that started down her face.

This man was going to kill all the people she loved. She gritted her teeth in righteous anger when it truly dawned on her that this man had killed her father. Her father was a great man and had earned his recognition in the medical field. He hadn't deserved to die.

She tried to keep her voice steady when she said, "First I want to say that you did deserve recognition for what you did in the war, Mr. Johnson, but why did you take my father's life when he could have saved so many people? Why did you think your life was more valuable than his?"

She could feel Johnson mellow a bit while he pondered her question. His grip lessened and the gun now pointed to the floor.

"Because if it wasn't for war veteran's like me, then your old man wouldn't have had the freedom to practice medicine in the first place."

Stanton cleared his throat and then said, "He's got a point, Maya. Then the fact that your father was a gypsy, too."

"That's right!" said Johnson, seemingly pleased that all agreed.

The phone fell off Eve's desk a second before Maya spit in Johnson's face. Then Maya twisted her body, scratched and hit at her captor with all her anger and might. She didn't really realize that Stanton joined in her struggle until she heard a bone snap.

Then the gun flew down with a crash on the floor.

"Everybody stand back!" It was Eve. She retrieved the gun, now holding it with two hands.

"Are you all right, Charles? Uh...C.J?"

"Yes, darling, I'm all right. It just looks like I'll have a sore arm is all."

Maya was dumbfounded. Eve's alliance seemed to still hold with Johnson.

Except for heavy breathing, everyone was quiet for what seemed like an eternity. Maya looked at Eve, then Stanton and last, Johnson.

"Eve, now you realize that he just knocked you out, don't you?" Maya asked.

"It was just part of the plan," Johnson said. "I love you, Eve, you know that." He started to rise, stretching a hand out to her. "Just give me the gun, sweetheart."

Eve slowly backed up to the door and reaching behind, opened it. When she looked out, Johnson quickly moved toward her and Stanton tripped him. When Johnson fell, he grabbed at Maya. She fell straight back and down, but managed to kick him in the face in the process.

"It's the police."

Maya heard and then saw them rush in, secure the gun from Eve and cuff Johnson. She turned away onto her stomach and cried against the floor because Johnson's greed had killed her father. Over the land he loved so much. Though she made the decision to keep the land her father had died for, now her commitment was more permanent. A bone-deep commitment. She'd keep it forever.

Maya felt a hand on her shoulder and jerked away, frightened.

"Maya, it's okay. It's all over," Stanton said.

Standing, she ran the back of her hand over her tears. "Yeah, it's all over."

"You did good, Maya. I knew that–I hoped that the spitting gypsy would come out eventually."

Maya smiled in response and surveyed the room. Sam appeared to be getting a statement from Eve. Outside, three police cars had lights flashing. C.J. Johnson sat in the back of one, head down. The vehicle started to back out, then moved away from the building. Maya sighed with relief.

"You probably haven't eaten anything all day, have you?" Stanton pulled her gaze back to him.

"I don't remember." She put a hand on her stomach and tried to focus. "No."

"Let's go get something then and get over to see Alice," he said gently.

Yes, Alice, she thought. Alice would be glad this was all over. Now finally, they could all heal up and get on with their lives. Stanton could–no.

Maya had been looking out the window again and noticed cars were slowly driving by. Soon the news would be out.

"Stanton, you've got to go. If this gets in the news, your life will become a circus. You must go. You can't be here when the press starts asking questions."

"But–"

"No. You must go. Now. I'll explain everything to Sam and the others. We'll keep you out of this and it'll be okay."

STANTON LOOKED OUT THE WINDOW NOW, TOO, REALIZING SHE WAS right. It would be a media frenzy, starting with the morning shows and continue for who knows how long. He felt Maya pushing from behind and he stopped only briefly, planting a kiss on her forehead.

"Thanks, Maya."

STANTON WAS GONE NOW, LEAVING HER JUST AS FAST AS C.J. HAD. Suddenly she felt like crying again. Sam headed her way and she tried to stop the flow with positive thoughts. Now she really could begin her life anew. With C.J. and Stanton out of her life and Alice on the mend, she had no other major stresses to deal with.

"You know you're lucky to be alive, young lady," Sam said. "You should have told me about this meeting. I'm not always so good at guesswork, you know. With some clues from Alice, I had a notion you'd be around here today."

"Yes, you're right. I'd planned to call you, but I was prevented.

Anyway, all's well that ends well. Was it the war, Sam, that did this to Mr. Johnson?"

"No. Over the years I've known vets who came back with one difficulty or another and haven't murdered anyone. Many good, honorable men came back from Vietnam. I'd also say that by the look and smell of him, he has a bad addiction to alcohol. It can damage the brain as well as the body.

Sam gave her a fierce hug.

She smiled up into his face. "Thank you."

"I just wished I could have helped you sooner. Glad you're all right, kid. I heard you tell Stanton you wanted him out of this. We'll honor your wishes, won't we, Ms. Dole?"

Eve stepped forward meekly. "Yes, of course. I have my own reasons for being quiet, too. To say the least, I've been duped by a crazy man. I don't want my business to be jeopardized in any way."

Maya was about to follow Sam out, when Eve touched her arm gently. "Please wait a second."

Eve looked like she was about to cry and it nearly made Maya crumble again.

"I'm very sorry," Eve said. "I really had no idea that Charles–C.J., was so mentally unstable. He was a man I cared about and sided with too deeply it seems. Now with newly opened eyes I've seen how mean I've been to you. I'm sorry. I only thought I was finally getting all I'd wanted. I was so wrong. I don't know what else to say."

Maya sighed. "You put the gun on Johnson, then opened the door to the police. I'd say that's enough."

Maya started to leave, but was stilled again by Eve's voice. "I do want to ask you, in a very professional manner, if you'd like to sell your property. I'd like to buy it to expand my holdings. Whatever price you're asking."

She would have laughed hysterically if it weren't for Eve's despondent face. "I can never sell my father's land. I'm sorry."

"Is that your final answer?"

"That's my final answer."

Eve patted her arm, then went to her desk and tore up the papers that Maya had signed. "Then I won't bother you about it again."

AFTER TALKING TO A LAWYER AND THE SHERIFF'S DEPARTMENT, MAYA decided not to have her father's body exhumed. C.J. Johnson still confessed with pride and those in her father's office testified to the fact that he was in the office at the time of death.

They did indeed make the news in Portland since her father was a notable physician. She was thankful she lived far away from the big city and that she was able to live a semi-private life here in Salisbury Junction.

No mention was made of Stanton Black being involved. Part of her was glad he avoided the media circus. Still, part of her resented that he had. The court said it would take a while until the case came to fruition.

She couldn't remember the last time her life was normal. Maybe it was before her father's death. She wished they could both rest in peace.

CHAPTER SEVENTEEN

The hospital didn't bill Maya for her stay. Afraid it might show as a negative on her credit report, she called the business office. The bill had been paid before she'd been released, the woman said. By a Mr. Stanton Black.

Although Maya appreciated his kindness, she couldn't accept the gift. Her tour guiding skills didn't warrant that kind of money. She had the office bill her insurance company instead. Then she had Alice take care of making sure the money went back to Stanton. She thought that the best route since he was in contact with Alice.

Before Maya knew it, her summer vacation passed and she'd had a moving company move her belongings from Portland.

She'd taken a substitute-teaching job at the high school, which would last until the current teacher came back from maternity leave. She'd been a lifesaver, they'd said.

Not only were they pleased with her, but the special education students in this town were behaviorally challenged to a lesser degree than in the big city, therefore she knew she'd have a relatively easy time teaching in Salisbury Junction.

On her way home from work, she stopped on Main Street to tour the shops. Alice's birthday was today and she had no clue what to get her.

Coming upon a bookstore, she stopped and looked in the window. To her surprise, she saw a neat arrangement of Stanton Black's newest book. Her feet seemed to move into the store with a mind of their own.

She picked one up, thinking it was the perfect gift for Alice. The picture on the back revealed that rare smile, making her wonder what, or who, caused it. She wished it could have been her, that she'd made some difference in his life. Obviously, she hadn't since she hadn't heard from him since he left.

Opening the book, she read the front flap. It was his usual, a suspense novel and no doubt a good read. Yes, Alice would enjoy this.

After she picked up two, she shook her head. It would be too tough to read Stanton's book, at least for the time being. She set one down, had the other gift-wrapped and departed for Alice's house.

"Oh my goodness," said Alice, with a hand on her heart. "You shouldn't have. I don't have birthdays anymore. I'm too old."

"Hey, you look a lot younger today than you have in the last six months. Besides, your life's just beginning."

"Yes it is," Alice said with a smile, ripping away the paper from her present. "Oh, Stanton's new book. He said it would be out soon."

Maya tried to smile, but was reminded that Stanton had been communicating with Alice, while she hadn't heard a word from him. It stung a little bit. A lot.

"Thank you very much. That reminds me, I received his latest work by registered mail this morning. It's on the desk, see? I'm to read it in one week's time, penciling in any historical errors. Life is good!"

Walking over to the desk, Maya picked up the manuscript. She tried to tell herself it was just out of curiosity since she'd never actually seen a manuscript before. But it was because writing was such a large part of Stanton's life.

"Turn to the dedication page, Maya. Look at what it says."

It was awkward to pick up, so she sat down at the desk. Alice now stood at her shoulder.

"To my Valentine," Maya read aloud. She had to catch her breath for a moment. In the next second she realized it could be to anyone and quite possibly to Michelle.

After total silence, Alice said, "Well? Aren't you touched that he's dedicated this book to you?" She picked up her new novel and opened it. "Look, he never dedicates his work to anyone. This has got to be a first."

Maya glanced at the novel Alice held, then back at the dedication.

"I know what you're thinking, Maya, that it could be anyone, but look the *V* is capitalized in Valentine. It's for you, honey."

Maya picked up a pencil from the desktop and circled the capital v as a mistake. Then thought better of it and crossed out the whole line.

"Oh no, Maya. Don't do that. You obviously mean a lot to him if he's dedicated this book to you."

She tossed down the pencil and turned abruptly. "Oh yeah, then why didn't he use my name? He didn't want to be seen with me when it really mattered. Like when the cameras were flashing."

Alice tried to touch her shoulder, but Maya squirmed, got up and stood by the window. "Stanton didn't like the limelight," Alice said in a quiet voice. "He didn't want his private life exposed for all to see."

"For Michelle to see, you mean."

"I don't think Michelle means much to Stanton. He didn't dedicate this book to her."

"Well it looks to me like he didn't dedicate this book to me, either. I'm sorry Alice, but it's not hard to spell Maya. My special education kids have had no problem with it."

Now Alice was wringing her hands. "I'm sorry you're so hurt, Maya. It's all my fault. Crazy me, but I thought that Stanton would be back and all would be well with the two of you. He hasn't come back but now after I've read this dedication, I'd hoped that–that you'd see that you were appreciated. Then I could feel better about using you to get to Stanton. That was wrong and I don't think I can apologize enough."

"Alice, never blame yourself. We did what we had to do at the time. That's all."

"No, that's not all. You did all you could do at the time. Yet, I didn't care about what you were going through, because I was dead set on working with Stanton. Your hurt is my fault. I'm responsible. The truth is, I don't deserve all the love and care you've shown me."

Alice had started crying and now Maya did, too.

"I'm not so stupid that I didn't realize you used me," Maya said. "But I've been so desperate for love, I just overlooked it for a sense of family. Still, I know you've always loved me and you see me as family. Well, we are family."

"Yeah, a dysfunctional family," Alice said and they both chuckled. "What family do you know that's not dysfunctional in some way?"

"Can't think of a one." Maya moved closer and they hugged fiercely.

"Do you know what, Maya? I need family just as much as you do. I'm alone, too."

Maya nodded.

"I'm glad we finally talked this out," Alice said.

Maya hadn't really thought that Alice needed her as much as she'd needed Alice. It was good to know.

WHEN MAYA LEFT FOR HOME, ALICE SAT DOWN WITH THE MANUSCRIPT and thought about what she hadn't told Maya. That Stanton asked about her often. Perhaps one day she would tell her, after time healed all wounds. Until then, some things were better left unsaid.

She erased the pencil marks on the dedication page and then added her own editing. It would be Alice's dedication as well as his. It now said: *To Maya Valentine.*

STANTON RECEIVED HIS MANUSCRIPT BACK FROM ALICE BEFORE THE allotted time and was pleased, anxious to see if he'd made any historical errors.

When he came across the dedication page he noticed something penciled in and eraser marks. He wondered what it could all mean. It looked like pencil marks made in anger and then erased. He wondered how his words could have made Alice mad. After all, the dedication page was a rather personal matter. Surely she knew that.

Realization struck and he knew what he'd done wrong. Even though the dedication made sense to him, it was too general. He supposed Maya could take it that way.

He'd counted on Alice to show her the dedication page and obviously, she had. That would explain the angry, original, pencil marks. Alice probably erased them and added her name.

While he rubbed his five o'clock shadow, he thought back to the times when Maya thought he didn't want others to know he was seeing her. She thought it was due to his relationship with Michelle Karr.

He knew now he should have explained his relationship with Michelle from the very beginning. Since he'd become famous he'd always kept his private live private. That was high priority. He'd learned the hard way that if you tell one person, you tell them all.

That's why he'd kept quiet since he'd last seen Maya, waiting for the Johnson trial to end. He was protecting her from a media circus, especially if Michelle got involved in it, too.

Even though he was dying to see Maya, he'd been strong, strong for them all. He took no chances, not even telephone calls. Nothing was going to trace him or Michelle to this case.

Stanton turned the page, concluding that Maya was a smart woman. The way she sent him out of Eve's real estate office before the press arrived confirmed it.

CHAPTER EIGHTEEN

*A*fter a mineralogist inspected the cave on her property, Maya thought it was rather humorous that the amount of gold that Johnson thought laid in wait at the back of her property was limited.

Her father dreamed of finding the gold that helped bring pioneers to this area over one hundred years ago. Not for monetary reasons, but for the recreation of it, poring over the earth with the search. She'd learn how to do this too, and pass this legacy on to her children one day as he would have.

By the time the murder case closed, she felt truly able to put it all behind her. With the passing of time she'd shed fewer tears over the loss of her father, a normal sign of grieving, Dr. Diethrick told her.

The person she couldn't get over was Stanton. In her mind's eye, she was forever trying to recapture the image of his face, the sound of his voice and the feel of his kiss.

On one sunny Saturday, Maya decided to return to California Gulch, the area that brought Stanton here in the first place. Since she'd never said a real goodbye to Stanton, she thought perhaps here in this monumental place she could say farewell and move on with her life.

She'd told Alice where she was going, having learned the hard way through the Johnson case that it was good to let others know your whereabouts. She packed a lunch, got Wonder Dog and drove off toward the mountains.

The deciduous trees, especially around the river, flaunted leaves in autumn tones of orange and red. Amongst the evergreens, the needles of the tamarack turned the color of rust. It looked different from when she and Stanton had been here. It had been so long ago that she worried she'd never be able to find "their" gulch again.

He was right, she realized. These areas needed to be marked. Through Alice, they would be. She had to admit she was a little jealous of Alice and her foundation, the connection she had with Stanton. Yet, too, she was happy for her success.

Now the area looked familiar and she parked her car at the road-block. Glancing around, she knew where she and Wonder Dog would head and slipped on her backpack.

Wonder Dog's tail was at a constant wag and he tried to keep pace with her while she climbed the hillside. He panted so hard, she hoped she'd not have to carry him. Finally, they made it to the top and she looked down at the beautiful scenery.

The first thing she focused on was the grassy knoll where Stanton had laid back and rested. She remembered his smile, how he playfully pulled her down onto him, and the wonderful hug he gave her. That was when he told her not to fear him.

That was her mistake, learning to trust him. To love a man that could not be there for her. She suffered a lot of hurt for that.

But he was a good man. He hadn't dismissed Alice when she was at death's door. He helped this spitting gypsy out of various scrapes along the way and charitably paid her hospital bill. Ultimately, he tried to save her from Charles Johnson. Then he was gone.

She wondered at what point he'd grown paranoid over publicity. Probably with his first book. It was just not easy for him to be open with the media. Somehow, he'd need to overcome this if he decided to marry Michelle. However, that was their problem, not hers.

"Goodbye and farewell, Stanton. I wish you happy and well. I hope you find peace and what you are looking for," she said and then shook her head to clear it. She threw a stick for Wonder Dog and then looked down. She tried to imagine the ghosts of the past, for she knew at one time the area swarmed with miners looking for a big break.

Yes, she thought she could almost imagine it and for a second she thought she'd heard a voice. It sounded like a male voice. Like Stanton's voice.

"Ghost of a chance," she said and then chuckled at herself for having such an obsession for him.

She heard it again, a human voice. Perhaps Wonder did too, since his ears perked. Then he barked.

A gripping chill caused her to realize she'd been scared once too often in this life. Always in the back of her mind would be the fear that somehow, some way, Johnson would be released and he'd find her.

Wonder Dog went back down the trail. She swore if she made it off this hill alive, she'd get a real watchdog. Touching her backpack, she realized she didn't even have a fork in her lunch for protection.

She steadied herself, thinking it was probably only a hiker. This was not the big city. This was out in nowhere, and security problems didn't often occur. She hated this feeling of fear, this pounding of her heart. What a curse to humanity was apprehension!

At last, Stanton spotted Wonder Dog and knew Maya was in the vicinity. He grew hoarse from calling her name, but nevertheless called out again.

After reaching California Gulch, he climbed the rise. When Maya recognized him, she ran forward and started to beat at his chest. He promptly grabbed both her wrists.

"How dare you scare me. How dare you come up here and scare me. How dare you mess with my life again!"

"It's okay, Maya. It's okay. I didn't mean to scare you. Really, I didn't. It's okay. Alice told me where I could find you."

He let go of her wrists and she put her arms around his waist.

Inside, where once denial flourished, a floodgate opened and she cried as she'd never cried before. She realized she'd needed him through Alice's illness, the loss of her father and through the murder case.

When the crying relieved the ache inside, she sobered. He'd not been there for her when she needed him most. The anger came quickly and she called him a pig in the bohemian language.

Stanton's eyebrows went down, then up, then down again. This time the language was not seductive to him. It served more as a slap across the face, as she'd intended.

"The murder case is over," he stated simply.

With hands on hips, she said, "Well, duh."

"I came back as soon as I heard."

If he thought he could just come back when the going was good, he had another thing coming. "For what?"

He was quiet for a moment, looking over the ridge. She could see his jaw clenching while he measured his words. "Well, for one, to live here. I thought you knew I wanted that."

She nodded. Somehow, after all this time, she'd thought he'd changed his mind. So now, her emotions ran a different course and she felt slighted because he hadn't said he'd come back for her. Slighted, then irritated.

"Why did you come looking for me? Do you need a tour guide or something?"

He shook his head and chuckled. Then he laughed and it echoed out into the wilderness. A joyous sound that she found irritating to say the least. She crossed her arms and turned her head away from him. No, she would not join in his laughter for the whole situation was just not that funny to her. She was up here in the first place to rid her life of this man, not to conjure him up.

He sobered quickly, looking at her frown and stance. "I came looking for you because this is what I'd planned all along. To come back to you."

"Why would you come back for me?"

"Because I love you. Remember, I told you back at the real estate office?"

She remembered and softened, but knew she shouldn't because she didn't trust him not to hurt her again. She tried to stand straighter. "Now, how would I know you love me since we've had no communication for the last–I don't know how many months?"

"I don't get this. You're the one who told me to leave. To leave before the media got to Eve's office."

"Yes, I remember." How could she forget, when she didn't even get a chance to say a real goodbye?

"Now I want you to know what I was thinking. Obviously, like you, I thought that this would be a media circus, but not just on my account. Another victim could be easily traced to me and that would be Michelle Karr."

She put up a hand. "Please, believe me, I don't want to hear about Michelle Karr."

"But, you must listen. I met Michelle when she wanted to buy the movie rights to my first book. I sold her the rights and then dated her about three times. Well, the media that follows me is nothing compared to the media that follows her. It's a horrible existence and I couldn't live like that, so I didn't pursue her any further. We were never serious."

"But I saw her on TV and she led the public to believe that the two of you are indeed serious."

He frowned. "Did you know that a movie star's marketability is gauged, among other things, by how many times they're on the cover of some magazine or have articles written about them? Michelle has been trying to seek as much publicity as possible and could get it with the public's interest in the two of us together. She knew I resented being used publicly this way but didn't really care, feeling justified to stretch the truth to help my book become a successful movie."

Maya nodded.

"I'm sorry, Maya. Alice helped me see that I ran when the going got rough. I can't do that anymore, honey, no matter the reason. I have to stand and fight and spit like a gypsy."

They both smiled. He stepped forward and kissed her nose.

Maya softened again. It was good to see him.

"I'm not going to run anymore," he said. "Although until today, I truly felt I had good reason to run from the Johnson case. Nevertheless, I should have been here for you. I promise from here on out I will be with you, hell or high water. You deserve nothing less. I found a place to rent in town. I have to leave again for a short while. My book is out and I have some minor promoting to do. Can't take too much of that, you know."

She liked what she heard, but they had a history and not always a good one. She just didn't think she could take watching him on television or reading about him in the newspaper, wondering when he would ever mention her.

She would be his little secret, his gypsy woman in the wilds of northeast Oregon.

Maya shook her head. "I don't think I can do this, Stanton. I can't live in a box. I have every reason to believe that's what it'll be."

Stanton frowned and Wonder Dog started barking at something over the ledge. They walked over to see Alice walking around their vehicles, wringing her hands.

Maya's eyes welled up with tears. She was very touched that Alice drove out to help. However, there was nothing she could do.

"She's worried about us," Stanton said. "I better go to her. Unless–"

It killed her to say goodbye to Stanton. "No, go. Please. I'd like some time alone here."

She watched him start down the hill, thinking that if he'd just stayed away, she would've been okay. Saying goodbye to a ghost was much easier. Now, alive in Salisbury Junction, she'd have to encounter him from time to time.

Her heart breaking, Maya turned and ran deeper into the forest. Wonder Dog was at her heels. She ran until it hurt, to feel pain somewhere else on her body besides her heart.

Suddenly she stopped, panting. She remembered she was a survivor. She'd gotten through the death of both of her parents and escaped death by a lunatic. She'd nursed Alice back to life. Now the two of them would get through this, too.

CHAPTER NINETEEN

*A*s customary, the morning news was on for background noise while Maya dressed for work. Bits and pieces usually caught her attention, but this morning she seemed focused on what she was doing until the peal of the telephone interrupted her.

"Maya, this is Alice."

"Oh, good morning, Alice."

"Yes, it is. I think."

"What do you mean, you think? What's the matter?" asked Maya.

"I have an interview with a newscaster. They want to know about the Foundation and I suppose how Stanton is connected to it."

"Do you want to do this interview?"

"Yes, yes I do. The history and the Foundation are number one to me and it's an excellent chance to inform the public about it. It's just that I have to be careful about what I say regarding Stanton. You know how he is with the press and all."

Maya knew very well. She could understand Alice's concern. "You should be okay if you just stick to the facts. I'd be careful not to give them anything they can run with, I suppose."

"Like what?" If Alice didn't sound concerned before she did now.

"I don't know. I don't mean to worry you. Just tell them about what you love. The history. The Foundation."

"The main reason I called is because I want you to come with me. I'd feel so much better if you'd come with me, maybe clear your throat if I say the wrong thing. You're my family and I need you at a time like this. I scheduled the meeting during your lunch break in hopes that you'd attend."

Maya supposed she could go with her and sit close enough to give her eye contact. "Sure, if it'd make you feel better, Alice. When is it?"

"Today."

Maya agreed and went to her closet in search of the perfect interview outfit. She knew she might have to sit next to Alice to get her through this.

When Maya reached the Foundation, she was surprised to see all the vehicles parked around the building. She had to drive down the street to find a parking spot and then came in the back door.

Inside the lights were so dim it took a moment for her eyes to adjust. She stood among others at the back and looked for Alice.

The sound of a familiar voice reached her. Stanton stood at a makeshift podium at the front of the room. Platform lights shone down on him. It did her heart good to see him. Like a breath of fresh air, she took in the sound of his voice and the expressions on his face. He looked considerably relaxed for doing a dreaded interview.

The interviewer was none other than Victoria Ott, top television journalist. Seeing this woman in the small town of Salisbury Junction helped Maya better understand the measure of Stanton's notoriety.

Stanton explained the plot of his new book. When the name Michelle Karr came up in the conversation, she backed into Alice standing next to the exit. Alice put a hand on her arm to steady herself.

Maya's heart plummeted thinking about the two of them together. The thought still hurt, making her wonder if she'd ever get over Stanton. Knowing Stanton, she doubted he'd divulge any information about Michelle. Even so, she wished she could leave this sensitive subject and go back to work. Unfortunately her agreement to stand by Alice until she finished her speech kept her riveted to the spot. She took a deep breath and held it, waiting for him to say something about Michelle.

"I'm not seeing Michelle Karr," he answered.

"Oh shucks, I thought we might get a top story on the two of you," said Victoria.

He smiled politely. "No, I'm really not seeing Michelle. We're not dating anymore. That was months ago."

Maya let her breath out.

"Well, ladies, now you've heard it from the horse's mouth, so to speak. He's available."

"Actually, I'm not."

"Oh? Top story?"

"Sure, why not," he said and leaned forward.

Victoria licked her lips and Maya felt sorry for him. She shook her head not believing that Stanton would offer any more personal information. She turned to the door, not wanting to hear about the woman he was dating, when she heard her name.

"Maya Valentine," he said.

"What was the name again, Stanton?"

"My–ah Valentine," he pronounced. "Cute name, huh?"

Maya felt Alice's hand tighten on her arm.

"Now is this the truth? You're not pulling my leg are you?" Victoria asked.

He sat up straighter. "No, this is the truth. I met Maya here in northeast Oregon while I was researching a book."

Maya couldn't believe her ears and looked at Alice's face for the first time. Alice smiled from ear to ear. "I didn't know he would be here," she said.

"She's a teacher," Stanton continued. "Oh, I have a picture of her."

The woman held the picture up to the camera. Maya recognized the picture as one she'd given to Alice. Maya and Alice both sniffed.

"She's beautiful," the woman said.

"Yes. Gypsy blood in her background."

"Sounds serious, Stanton."

Someone in the audience sneezed, drawing Stanton's attention away from Victoria. When his eyes connected with Maya's, his eyebrows rose in surprise. He didn't look away from her when he said, "We've had some setbacks. Her father was murdered. She's gone through some tough times. I plan to marry her and be there for her, if she'll have me."

Clearly, Stanton was a changed man. He wasn't going to hide his gypsy woman in the wilds of northeast Oregon, after all.

He mentioned her father's death so he must be prepared to face any questions a journalist might ask.

Alice handed her a tissue and Maya dabbed at her eyes. If her heart was any lighter, she'd be floating around the room like a balloon.

"I didn't know," Alice said again. "But how wonderful, just the same."

Stanton and Victoria stood and shook hands and then a man stepped forward. "Time to set up for Alice Roberts."

"Oh, it's my turn," Alice said and took a deep breath. "I believe I can say anything I want to now. You wait here, dear."

Stanton gave a hug to Alice in passing. He turned and gave the group of people a quick perusal, then caught sight of Maya. He searched her face. When she smiled, he approached her.

When he took her in his arms, she felt the weight of the world fall from her shoulders, replaced by peace and joy. A flash from a camera broke the spell and she saw that people were trying to get Stanton's attention.

Stanton raised his hand in a signal for silence. "Maya and I will answer your questions right after Alice gives her interview."

ABOUT THE AUTHOR

MARY VINE is an author, publisher, speaker and retired educator. She writes contemporary and historical romantic fiction, a time travel series, and inspirational children's books. Mary, and her husband can usually be found in Southwest Idaho or Northeast Oregon. www.au-thormaryvine.com

    If you enjoyed reading the book, please leave a review. It is the best way to thank an author.

ALSO BY MARY VINE

CONTEMPORARY ROMANCE

Maya's Gold

A Place to Land

Secrets of Trillium Falls

Snake River Rendezvous

HISTORICAL ROMANCE

Wanting Moore

TIME TRAVEL SERIES

Nugget of Time

Goldbrick

Summer Solstice

INSPIRATIONAL CHILDREN'S BOOKS

The Big Guy Upstairs

Biju Silver Lining

Dragon Gilby

Dragon Gilby and Jamie Deer

www.ingramcontent.com/pod-product-compliance
Lightning Source LLC
Chambersburg PA
CBHW030452250626
47154CB00003BA/1238